# Mind Over Matter

*many*
*Enjoy the read!*

## S.J. Clarke

MuseItUp Publishing
www.museituppublishing.com

Mind Over Matter© 2011 by S.J. Clarke

MuseItUp Publishing
14878 James, Pierrefonds, Quebec, Canada, H9H 1P5
http://www.museituppublishing.com

Cover Art © 2011 by Delilah K. Stephans
Edited by Gloria Oren
Copyedited by Susan Davis
Layout and Book Production by Lea Schizas

P-ISBN: 978-1-927085-96-7
Production by MuseItUp Publishing

# MIND OVER MATTER

♦

## S.J. CLARKE

# Dedication

This book is dedicated to the memory of Colleen Panteah, who coaxed, prodded and shoved until I agreed to write for her. This woman, stronger than any I've ever known, refused to allow the writer in me to cower.

Thank you, Frodo, for encouraging me to live my dream. I am forever grateful.

# Acknowledgements

I am surrounded by people who support and inspire me.

To my editors, Gloria Oren and Susan Davis, this book is so much better as a result of your efforts. Thank you is not enough.

To The Writers' Community of Durham Region (WCDR), a group of dedicated writing professionals always there to exchange knowledge, and to offer help and support to writers of all levels—I thank you for embracing a shiny, novice, would-be writer with confident enthusiasm.

To the organizers of The Ontario Writers' Conference (OWC)— thank you for the opportunity to continue to learn while giving back to the writing community. Your talents and spirit draw out the best in me. I'm honoured to be a part of this amazing organization.

To WIP, my critique group, who offered up decadent treats with insightful suggestions, (and to those who are wondering, yes, a bucket full of sugar helps the medicine go down)—you all rock!

To Paula Hargraves, best friend extraordinaire, there with a pat on the back, or a kick in the ass, whichever she deemed appropriate for the occasion—you always look out for me. From first seed to finished story, you offered perceptive recommendations and well-timed encouragement. Thank you!

To my family, those people who learned to live with a wife and mother only half-present through the writing, revision, and editing of this book—thank you for staying positive, even when I didn't. I love you all.

# Chapter One

Three years ago, Rebecca's daughter disappeared. Most people thought Sabrina was dead. When they ran into Rebecca, they didn't know what to say, or how to treat her anymore, as though her identity had been stolen along with her child. Jenna Cowling nodded in the grocery store, unable to meet Rebecca's eyes or hide the pity in her own. Donald Rumsford, the pharmacist over on Grand, peered over glasses wedged on the end of a bulbous nose. Rebecca knew he wondered if the drugs in the bag were all that kept her going.

Every weekend, on her way into town, Rebecca stopped in to see Chief Bains, hoping to hear news of a fresh lead. Anything. And each week she fought to swallow the pain when he sighed and shook his head.

Old Jim Grimley sat on his front porch swing, watching the same things on Main Street happen day after day. He pushed off with his foot and muttered that Ms. Rebecca was goin' to have to face facts.

On Saturdays, when Rebecca sat alone in the corner booth at Ruby's Diner, the same booth she and Sabrina always ate breakfast in, the other regulars glanced over, leaned their heads close together and whispered to one another.

"Sad, so sad," they said. "She isn't quite right since her baby girl disappeared." Then they went back to their regular meals and normal routines and pushed their plates aside, like they could push aside their discomfort, so the ugliness of the truth couldn't touch them.

"Mornin' Becca," Ruby said, grabbing the pencil tucked into her nest of bleached curls and the order book from her apron pocket. "Your usual?"

"Good morning," Rebecca said, smiling, "Yes. That would be great. Thanks."

"Be right back with your coffee."

Rebecca set her purse on the bench seat and looked around the diner. Orange vinyl and cracked linoleum didn't deter people for long. Ruby's food boasted a reputation of its own. A decent sized crowd graced the diner for this early in the day, Rebecca noted, a few strangers and the usual Saturday morning crew. Donna Mayhew, head bent over the latest best-seller, ate her bacon and tomato on toast, well done—without looking up from the page. Norman Parks coughed into his monogrammed hanky, then placed it, neatly folded, back into his pocket. He peered at his special order of poached eggs, nodding his approval before shaking the paper napkin out and draping it across his lap. Joshua Bishop rubbed his belly while savoring the last of his coffee and smiled a greeting at Rebecca. *We're all such creatures of habit. The same people, ordering the same food as last Saturday, sitting at the same tables.*

Turning her attention to the weekly paper she carried, Rebecca scanned the headlines, ready to read about the latest happenings in Cutter's Gulch, Arizona. She probably heard about them already, given that in a small town, news flew between lips faster than print could meet paper.

"Stolen car abandoned in Wilmott Creek, local teens suspected." "Blood Donor Clinic at Town Hall Saturday 10-2." "Friends of the Library used book sale next week." Just as she thought, old news.

"What excitin' plans have you got for today?" Ruby asked, setting the coffee cup and saucer and a small tureen of milk on the table.

"Just finished a contract this morning. I think I'll give myself a bit of a break before starting the next..." A family of six came in, eager tourists gearing up before heading out to Wanagi Peak and the ghost town at the base.

"Hold that thought." Ruby chuckled as she headed over to grab a booster seat for the enthusiastic toddler trying to escape his mother's hand.

Rebecca set the paper down to reach for the milk. Her forearm hit the paper, knocking over the tureen.

"Well, damn." She jumped back as far as possible and used her paper napkin to mop up the spill, while trying to get Ruby's attention. Ruby, her hands full taking orders, didn't notice. Eyeing the workstation around the corner from the booth, Rebecca got up and grabbed a cloth and the milk carton, still sitting on the counter. She refilled the tureen, sat down, and added the milk to her coffee.

"Ahhhh," she said, smiling. "Still nice and hot." About to return the milk to the counter, Rebecca saw the photo of a missing child on the side of the carton, and her vision blurred as the familiar pain stabbed at her temples. She pressed her hands on both sides of her head, but it did nothing to alleviate the pressure. "Oh my God," she whispered. "They're back!"

Rebecca scooted over as far as she could to hide in the depths of the corner booth, grateful that other customers kept Ruby busy. Rebecca knew from experience she didn't have much time left. A vision came at her, hard and strong...

*The child's face from the milk carton, about six or seven years old, hovered before her, similar yet different. Shivers wracked her body as she huddled in a corner, her long brown curls limp and dull. Smudges on her face spread when she used a dirty forearm to swipe away tears, and a cut bled through the tear in her dress. A flickering light illuminated the dark room, hinting at secrets in the shadows. The sound of water dripping, slow and steady like a leaky faucet, met Rebecca's ears and her nose crinkled at the stench of urine and human waste. The child looked up. All trace of color drained from her face when a deep voice crept out of the darkness.*

*"It's time."*

"Rebecca, did you hear me?" Ruby's voice penetrated the fog surrounding Rebecca's mind.

"W-What?" She lifted her head, taking in the dining room around her. The tourist family still sat waiting for their breakfast. "I'm sorry Ruby, what did you say?"

"You okay, hon? You were in another world there for a minute."

"I'm fine. Really," she added at Ruby's doubtful expression. "Didn't sleep well again last night, I guess." She forced a grin. "Good thing you caught me before I nodded off and started drooling in my coffee." The mention of coffee drew Rebecca's gaze to the carton of milk again. The girl's innocent face stared back. Something seemed wrong. Rebecca leaned in, reading the caption under the photo. Nicole Wilson; missing for six years, before Bree even.

"I hope you don't mind that I helped myself to the milk," Rebecca said, and explained what happened. "Didn't want to be a bother."

"Honey, it's no problem at all, but you didn't have to do that."

"Not to worry, it's over and done now." Rebecca looked down at the pancakes and fruit before her and knew little would make it past her lips "Breakfast looks delicious, as usual," she lied.

Ruby looked over at the children's order of pancakes in front of the empty seat across from Rebecca. She moved her gaze back to Rebecca for a moment longer, before nodding as if confirming something in her head. "Okay then. Enjoy." Ruby picked up the milk carton as a bell dinged from the kitchen area. "Let me know if you need a refill on your coffee." Smiling, Ruby went off to deliver the next order.

Rebecca's stomach roiled at the thought of eating. Nausea and a headache overwhelmed her. She needed to get home where she could decipher what this vision meant. With Ruby monitoring her every move, coming up with a way out of the diner proved difficult.

Forcing another smile, Rebecca picked up her fork and knife and waved them in the air for Ruby to see. At Ruby's disappointed frown, Rebecca cut the pancakes, and placed a small piece between her lips. Once Ruby smiled and turned away, Rebecca spit the bite out into a napkin. She spent another few minutes cutting and moving food around, hiding small bits under the second pancake. Pulling some money out of her wallet, she kept an eye out. As soon as Ruby went back to the kitchen for the next order pick-up, Rebecca threw the bills down on the table and made her escape.

Rebecca's first deep breath came when she sat safe inside her car at the other end of Main Street. Home. She had to hold it together until then. Shoving the key into the ignition, she crossed her fingers, and then groaned at the dull grind that met her ears.

"Crap. Not today!" Rebecca cursed for putting off taking the car in to Joshua. Hands shaking, she tried again, holding her grimace until the engine caught.

The edge of another vision crept in while she pulled into the driveway. "Shit. One more minute, come on, one more minute."

She fumbled at the keyhole, hands shaking too hard to fit the key in the lock. Rebecca crossed the threshold and fell to her knees as the pain sliced in again, worse this time. Never before had two visions come so close together. What the hell?

Rebecca's world faded and in its place…

*Sabrina appeared. Her baby. Sitting on the floor in a room of shadows, chin resting on drawn up knees. "Where are you Mommy? Why haven't you come?" The shadows opened up, pushing forward to swallow both the light and Bree.*

"Noooooooooo." Rebecca came back tears streaming down her face and fell to the floor. Limp, she laid there, an arm thrown across her eyes. *"So close."*

Rebecca rolled as her stomach revolted, giving up its meager contents. Pushing herself to her knees with the last heave, she drew the back of a hand across her mouth.

The memory of losing Sabrina burned in her mind forever, but these fresh images; God, they made it so much worse. Rebecca crawled the few feet to the still open door, shoved it closed and leaned against it, shaking with sobs.

The late morning sun shone through the windows when she refocused. Struggling to her feet, she took in the scene around her.

*Clean this mess up, and then shower. You can deal with the rest later.* Rebecca tossed the soiled clothes in the washing machine on the way to the bathroom.

Revived by the hot shower, Rebecca poured a glass of iced tea. She curled up in the big chair in the living room, rested her chin on her knees, and tried to make sense of the morning's events. Break it down. Concentrate on one thing at a time. Tackle the vision at Ruby's first.

*Who are you, Nicole Wilson, and why are you in my head?* Rebecca pulled her laptop over and clicked on the missing-children database icon on the screen. A quick search brought up the case page. Nicole Wilson of Sacramento, taken six years ago last month, would have been nine on her next birthday. The authorities classified her case as a stranger abduction.

Rebecca sipped her iced tea, rolling an ice-cube in her mouth, and pondered the similarities to Bree's case. She didn't believe in coincidences.

Both were girls, taken by strangers, three years apart, at roughly the same age. Was it possible these kidnappings were connected? A staggering two thousand children go missing every day in the United States alone. These two cases might have nothing to do with one another. Nothing, that is, except for showing up in her visions, on the same day.

And Bree. God, Rebecca, allowed fragile hope to emerge. Her baby girl looked good. Unlike Nicole, Bree appeared healthy and clean. Older. "Oh my God, Bree looks older! The way she'd look standing here today." Rebecca's face dropped into her hands, as tears flowed. "She's alive."

# Chapter Two

Rebecca stared at the building in front of her as she smacked the steering wheel.

"Damn it!" She didn't want to be here. It galled her to ask for help from the very man who gave up on the search for Bree. But she didn't see another option. For Sabrina's sake she had to go in and convince the sorry son-of-a-bitch to put her daughter's case back on the top of his ever-present to-do list.

Today Rebecca was facing facts. The dreams had returned, showing Bree as she looked today. God, seven already. The image made Rebecca's heart swell and her breath catch. Her beautiful baby. Sandy brown curls framed a face free of the pudgy swell of baby fat. She'd even lost a tooth. Not one of the front and center teeth most kids lose first, but an eyetooth. Rebecca thought ahead to Bree's seventh birthday next month. Every September Rebecca made a cake, lit the candles, and wished the same wish, but could never quite bring herself to eat a piece. This year Rebecca vowed she and Bree would blow out the candles together and eat until their bellies burst.

Her visions didn't lie. Sometimes they took unusual twists and turns, and often she had to look deep to see it, but they always led to a truth. Bree lived. Rebecca knew it to be a fact, and she intended to bring Sabrina back with a little help from Agent Cooper.

Rebecca went looking for the team lead of the Child Abduction Rapid Deployment unit, only to find Agent Dan Cooper no longer worked with the Bureau. Rebecca wondered if he lost his connections with his title. She needed Agent Cooper. He knew the case. Hell, he all but took up residence in Sabrina's room looking for clues, trying to get inside the head of the maniac who took her. He knew Sabrina, and he knew Sabrina's mother.

Dan Cooper and his team investigated both Rebecca and Pete, examined every detail of their lives until they were convinced neither parent had anything to do with their daughter's abduction. Opening herself up to scrutiny again didn't worry Rebecca.

What made Rebecca reluctant to walk into that building and ask Cooper for help had more to do with what he knew about her other life. The life where visions snaked through her mind, twisting, and striking when she least expected it. The life where she loses control to a power she doesn't understand and can't explain. Agent Cooper knew about her journeys into her alternate reality. Knew about them, but brushed them off, blaming emotional trauma as the cause of her nightmares.

He could deny it all he wanted, but she recognized the signs. He made a connection to Bree while sitting alone in her room for hours at a time. Rebecca was convinced Dan held the key to finding her daughter.

Aside from his psychic connection to Bree, Dan remained the only member of the team to not shoot looks of pity at her, the desperate mother who'd say anything to make them keep looking for her child. Cooper stayed focused on the search without getting his emotions involved, neither believing nor pitying. He did the job full out until he made the decision to stop.

No one called it a cold case or admitted to exhausting all leads. They assured her the search continued, but from headquarters. As each day passed, contact lessened. Daily reports became monthly phone calls. Before long, communication only happened when Rebecca made it happen.

A wave of heat blasted her when she opened the car door, seeping through the soles of her shoes as she walked toward the building. The air-conditioned interior did little to calm her nerves, or her temper.

Terrazzo marble floors led to a bank of elevators with a tenant listing posted to the left. Rebecca found Anderson Security, Inc. listed as Suite 804. *Breathe, just breathe.* Swiping her sweaty palms on her thighs, Rebecca stepped off the elevator and turned right until she came to the small brass plaque announcing Anderson Security.

Warm textured browns covered the walls. Tan Berber carpeted the floors and photographs of the local landscape hung throughout. A small seating area with four comfortable chairs and a pair of round tables, each big enough to hold a cup of coffee, but not much else, sat in front of the reception desk. The office looked deserted, Rebecca thought. Sounds of a muffled voice made her jump and almost knock the lamp off the side table. She followed the murmur, along the corridor off the reception area, until she came to the open door.

Rebecca leaned against the door jam and waited, arms crossed, while he finished his call. His dark hair brushed the collar of the casual blue shirt covering a white T-shirt. He looked good. *Wow, where had that come from?* She ignored the tingle starting low in her belly and pulled her mind away from dangerous ground.

"Thanks. I appreciate the heads up," Dan said. "And Michael? You don't have anything to make amends for. Understood? Great, take care." Dan hung up. "Rebecca." He nodded. "Come in."

She straightened and stepped away from the doorway, frustrated to feel on the defensive so early in this meeting. "I didn't mean to eavesdrop," she said, biting her lower lip.

Dan smiled in that way of his. It always managed to get on her nerves, not so small it appears ingenuous, but not so big it deflects from the solemnity of the occasion. A skill he learned in his years with the Bureau, no doubt.

"Sit." Dan waved his hand toward one of the chairs opposite his desk. "Can I get you something?" One eyebrow rose. "Iced tea, sweetened, right?"

Nothing wrong with his memory. "No, thank you." Rebecca inclined her head toward the phone. "You have spies on me?"

He flashed his signature smile again. "The team and I keep in touch. We're still close. You can't work the job together and not be." His expression turned serious. "What brings you by?"

"Why did you leave the Bureau?" she countered.

"An opportunity to work with friends I respect and admire presented itself." Dan sighed when Rebecca simply raised her brows. "Let's just say I needed a change."

"So you just left?" Her jaw dropped. "That's becoming a habit with you. At least the others make a pretense of looking. But you? You abandoned her. Is that what they teach at the Bureau? To walk away when a case gets difficult?" She stood. "I should never have come here."

"Sit down, Rebecca." Dan pulled a bottle of water out of the mini fridge concealed in the mahogany cabinet behind him. Rounding the desk, one hand pressed the bottle into her hands while the other applied a light pressure on her shoulder until she sat again. She held her breath, until the warmth of his hand disappeared. "Sabrina's case is still very much active. The search didn't stop just because I left." He sat on the edge of the desk and crossed his legs at the ankles. "Contrary to how it looked when I moved the team back to the Phoenix office, I never stopped caring. My contacts at the FBI have promised to let me know of any new leads that come in," he paused until her eyes met his again "and I've been doing some investigating on my own."

"Why? You claim you've moved on. If the FBI is still looking, as you claim, why continue searching out leads?" She held his gaze with her own, willing him to admit to the connection he shared with Bree. "Or is there something you're not telling me?" Bingo. A brief flicker in the depth of his eyes gave him away.

Dan crossed his arms over his chest. "You've learned to fight in the last three years."

"I had to. I'm the only one fighting to find her," Rebecca's voice cracked. "It's why I came here."

"I know it's hard. One new lead could turn it around; something to make us look at things in a different way. I can't quite get them to fit yet, but the pieces are there, I can feel it."

She looked away to gather her courage, then met his eyes and said what she knew he didn't want to hear, "I've seen Sabrina."

"What! Where?" He moved around the desk and reached for the phone before she could blink. "Tell me everything you know."

"In a vision."

He put the phone down. "Rebecca," he sighed.

"I'm not having nightmares Dan and I'm not crazy." She slapped her hand on the desk. "This is real, dammit. I saw Sabrina. Sitting on the floor of a dark room," Rebecca swallowed hard, "calling for me. Every vision appears for a reason. You said you needed a fresh lead. I've just handed you one."

"Even if I believed you, a chair in a dark room isn't much to go on. It's been three years; chances are she's no longer there."

She smiled at him. "That's just it. It wasn't a vision of Sabrina from back then." Rebecca took pity at his confusion. "It's from where she is now."

Rebecca saw a glimmer in Dan's eyes. She had his attention. Now to get him to believe her.

"Let me tell you what happened. Promise me you'll keep an open mind." Dan shook his head even as he opened his mouth to speak, but she cut him off before he could say no. "Just listen, that's all I'm asking. If you can't or won't help me, after hearing what I have to say, then I'll walk out of here and never bother you again."

He remained silent for so long Rebecca thought she misjudged him, until he sat down and leaned back in his chair.

"Tell me what happened," he said, crossing his arms over his chest. "And don't leave anything out."

She told him everything, except the part about being sick afterward.

He leaned forward at the end, resting his forearms on the desk. "You're telling me another child is involved? Held captive with Sabrina?"

"I don't know, maybe. I'm not sure if she's with Bree. There's a reason I had both visions back to back. The circumstances were so similar, you know. Both were girls, both almost the same age when they disappeared, though Nicole is a few years older than Bree now. They even resemble one another. The connection is there, but I need your help to find it."

Rebecca searched Dan's face, trying to read him.

"I know you want to hear I believe in your visions," he said, at last. "I wish I could say I do, but I'd be lying." Dan held up a hand to hold off her comments. "My turn to talk now," he continued. "What I will do is look into Nicole Wilson's case. Missing Persons stopped using milk cartons long ago, but a few states have started them up again. My first step is to—"

"Our," she corrected.

The muscles in Dan's jaw clenched.

"We need to get something clear from the start. I'm here to hire you. By agreeing, you'll report to me. I refuse to sit on the sidelines again, and I won't be the victim—or anything else. This time I need to know everything, no exceptions. This is my daughter's life. I can't have it any other way." She held out her right hand. "Do we have a deal?"

"I haven't agreed to take you on as a client yet." Her hand fell to her side. "I'll help you with this, but I'm not taking your money."

"It's the only way this will work."

Silence hung in the air. "I have a few things I need from you as well."

Rebecca's head tilted as she considered his request. She cleared her throat. "All right, fair's fair. What?"

"We may be working as a team, but I'd be in charge." He raised his hand, cutting off unspoken protests. "If we're in a dangerous situation, if it even borders on questionable, I need to know you'll react without hesitation and do as I say. We can argue about it later all you want." Dan sighed at her silence. "I can't do my job if I'm worrying about your safety."

Rebecca nodded. "I can try to do that." His right eyebrow rose. "Fine, I can do it," she snapped.

"Good. I need you to understand I'm going into this with a solid, scientific approach."

"Meaning?"

"Just because I'm willing to listen to your version of these visions doesn't mean I'm buying into them." His voice gentled, "I happen to think your visions are your mind's way of dealing with a very difficult situation." His hand extended. "It's the only way this will work for *me*. Do we have a deal?"

She let out the breath she held. He'd have no choice but to believe when the visions played out. Rebecca placed her hand in his. A tingle ran up her arm, and she jerked, eyes widening in dismay.

"Deal. Where do we go from here?"

He reached for the phone. "We learn everything we can about Nicole Wilson."

# Chapter Three

Dan nursed his beer while he waited for Rebecca. O'Gradey's was winding down. The after-work crowd headed out, and the Friday evening crew had yet to arrive. He smiled at the antics of one frisky couple in the corner whose inhibitions lowered with the level of beer in their glasses.

"Hey Dan, can I get you another one?"

Dan grinned. "I'm fine for now, Val, thanks. You might consider getting a couple more cold ones for those two over there, though."

Her brow furrowed. "Looks like John and Tina have had plenty already."

"It's over their heads you should be pouring them, I'm thinking."

Val laughed, "Might be worth it to see the looks on their faces, don't you know?" With a wink, she set off for her next table.

Val and her husband Jack ran O'Gradey's together. The family pub offered decent food, great service, and a good atmosphere. The music was loud and the lighting low.

When covering simple logistics, the team frequently held their weekly update meetings here, rather than in the conference room at the office, and usually ate at the same time. They sat in a small section off to the side intended for private groups. It worked for them, secluded enough to have a conversation without worrying about eavesdroppers. Of course, when looking for real privacy he wouldn't hold a meeting in a bar, but for today's purposes, it suited him fine.

A shaft of sunlight pierced the dark interior of the room, giving the new arrival a mysterious silhouette. Dan recognized Rebecca's lean bodylines even before his eyes adjusted. He stood, and she headed in his direction.

"Did you learn any more about Nicole?" Rebecca asked, taking the chair opposite him.

"Yes, but I'm waiting for Michael to get back to me on a few things."

"It's been a week since he returned from his last case. Shouldn't he have something for you by now?" Rebecca flopped back in the chair. "I see nothing much has changed. The Bureau still takes its sweet time doing things once a case drops off the radar."

Dan watched Rebecca's eyes linger on his beer before she ordered a sweetened iced tea. Leaning forward, Dan willed her eyes to meet his. "I know you're anxious to get started, to physically get out, and do something to find Sabrina. We'll get there, I promise. If we don't do some groundwork first, we won't have a direction to go in."

"Why is it taking so long? When Sabrina disappeared it seemed like answers came right away, at least to some of the questions."

He sighed. "For every member of the team you saw, a dozen more raced behind the scenes following leads, doing background checks and gathering information so we could focus on our jobs in the field. This time, it's just you and me, at least for now. Be patient."

"It's been three years, haven't I been patient enough?"

"Don't expect a CSI investigation. There's no glamor, just a lot of good old fashioned legwork, and more waiting." She rolled her eyes and he hid a smile. "Once we have the information we need, we can move forward with the next step of the plan," he took a sip of his beer and paused while Val dropped off Rebecca's tea, "which is why we're here tonight."

"Right. What exactly is the next step of the plan? You insisted this meeting take place here. Why?" She picked up her glass and waited.

"I have a proposal for you."

Her brows drew together. "What kind of proposal?"

"Marriage."

Rebecca froze. "That's a bit extreme, don't you think?" She took a long drink of tea.

"No, actually, I don't."

Rebecca sputtered as she struggled to get the mouthful down. She wiped her face with the paper napkin and stared at him. "You're kidding, right?"

"No." Dan watched her jaw drop and chuckled. Rebecca's jaw moved up and down, but no sound came out. "We pretend to get engaged," he clarified, "which provides a plausible explanation for me moving in with you." He sipped his beer and watched her process his words.

"I don't think moving in is necessary." The muscles along her throat contracted. *Christ, does the thought of being close to me scare her that much?*

"We'll be spending a lot of time together. Driving back to Phoenix every night would be a waste of time and gas. Besides, it's better if people think we're engaged."

"Why the pretense?"

"I don't want anyone to know what we're doing, or even that you've started looking for Sabrina again." Dan waited for his implication to register.

Rebecca gasped and leaned closer. "But that would mean you suspect someone in Cutter's Gulch of kidnapping Sabrina," she whispered. "Who, for God's sake? You looked at everyone three years ago."

"I don't have a suspect right now. To be more precise, everyone is a suspect until I've eliminated them." Dan kept his voice low, calm. "I don't want to advertise why I'm in town. People will get suspicious, clam up, even if they had no part in it." Doubt lingered in her eyes. "It's a natural reaction, given the amount of time that's passed. They'll wonder what's happened to change things." Dan played his trump card. "Are you prepared to reveal your new lead to your friends and neighbors?"

Rebecca turned her head away, and then looked back at him. "You know the answer to that. They already think I'm crazy, I'm not about to hand people another reason to question my sanity."

"Okay then," Dan said. "We'll say we're engaged."

"No one will believe it."

"Why?"

"I don't have what you'd call an active social life." He heard the sharpness in her voice, and knew it burned her to admit it. "I can't just show up one day announcing my engagement."

"You've already laid the groundwork by coming into Phoenix several times in the last month. How have you explained that to people?"

Rebecca tilted her head to the side. "It hasn't come up. I doubt if anyone's even noticed."

Dan shook his head. "A person can't get a parking ticket in Cutter's

Gulch without half the town buzzing about it. People have noticed your trips here, trust me on this."

Rebecca nodded. "You're right, not much slips past my neighbors. I just haven't heard about it. Yet." She chewed her bottom lip and tapped her nails on the table, nervous habits he recognized from her past. "But engaged? I don't think I could sell it."

"Whatever it takes to get Sabrina back."

Her eyes snapped. "If it had a chance of working. Your plan needs rethinking." The tap-tap-tapping of her nails ended when Rebecca sat back in her chair, arms crossed.

"It'll work," Dan insisted. "Three years is a long time, people expect you to move on. You're a private person, or you would have told people about coming out here. It's not that far of a stretch that you'd come here to meet a man. It's hard to keep a secret in Cutter's Gulch. It makes perfect sense you would want to start a new relationship away from prying eyes."

She leaned forward again. "But with you?"

Dan leaned back. "What's wrong with me?"

"Nothing," Rebecca said. "Everything." She threw up her hands. "You and your team weren't my favorite people when you left. I had no problem expressing my feelings to whoever would listen. You took the brunt of it." Her eyes welled. "You left Bree alone out there."

"I never..."

Rebecca sighed and averted her eyes. "That's not the point here, I know that. The people closest to me know I haven't been seeing anyone. Carrie for sure, I tell her everything."

"Even best friends get kept out of the loop on occasion. It's a big deal and out of character for you. You'd want to avoid explanations until you couldn't do so any longer. Given it's me, a lot of explaining may be required. Avoiding conflict is in character for you."

"Like you being a pompous jerk is in character for you?"

He hid a wince and tried not to squirm under her pointed stare. Maybe he pushed too far.

"You'd be surprised how much conflict I can stir up when I want to."

"I don't doubt it. You've become quite tenacious. Use that to your advantage. Make people believe we're together."

She stared at him so long this time he knew for sure he pushed her too far. "I can't do the engagement thing. It's too far out there for me. I dated Pete for three years before we got engaged and waited another two years to get married." She shook her head. "If you have to be there, why not as a live-in lover?"

Images appeared in Dan's head. *Rebecca under him, legs wrapped around him.* He shook his head clear. Thoughts like that are what distracted him three years ago. He'd made one of the biggest mistakes of his career because of it. He didn't plan to go down that road again. "I beg your pardon?"

"A lover serves the same purpose. I'm not a naive virgin. You said people expect me to move on." Rebecca shrugged her shoulders. "Let's give them what they expect and they won't see the real reason you're there. I can fake it if you can."

"And you'd be comfortable with people's reactions, what they might say?"

"Isn't that the point?" Rebecca asked. "To get a feel for what's going on in their heads? Nothing gets small towns talking like a bit of juicy gossip. And people won't hesitate to let me know how they feel to my face." Rebecca looked away. "Criticizing my choices isn't new to them." Dan saw the brief flare of hurt. "To answer your question, I have no problem with you posing as my lover."

"That's the plan then. I'll make a few arrangements and move in tomorrow."

Her eyebrows shot up. "You don't waste time, do you?"

"You said you were tired of waiting."

"All right. I'll get the guest room ready. It's my home office now, but there's a pull-out sofa in there. I guess I should call Carrie and let her know what's up."

"You can't tell anyone about this not being real." His eyes met hers. "Not even Carrie. I want to see people's reactions for myself. Why don't I just move in and see how long it takes others to notice."

"I hope you know what you're doing. Carrie's smart, she's going to know something's up."

"That's fine, let her speculate, but if she asks about us, you have to stick to the story."

"Which is?"

Dan thought for a moment as he finished his beer. "You come to Phoenix often enough for a day of shopping. We'll say we ran into each other one day, had coffee together to get caught up, and found we couldn't keep our hands off one another."

"Unlikely," she said with a laugh.

Twinges of disappointment at her quick refute surprised Dan. "The short story is we ran into each other and one thing led to another. We've spent several weekends together, and things are good. Living together is the next step. That should cover it. Anyone who wants more information will just have to ask. Give me your impressions on the key people in town," Dan continued.

"All of them?"

"Start with people who make it a point to stay in touch with you, those you interact with on a weekly basis. Then we'll cover the ones who've kept their distance. I still have access to my files from the case, so I have my perspective. I want to hear your viewpoint now."

"I can't even begin to imagine my friends as suspects. Carrie's my rock, my go-to person on the dark nights."

"They don't have to be suspects in your mind. Start with people who haven't let the circumstances change your relationship," Dan said. "Aside from Carrie, who else comes to mind?"

Rebecca sighed. "I don't have a lot of close friends. I've known Carrie since grade school, and a few other people around town I get together with once in a while. Most of my friends got jobs out of state. The few college friends I keep in touch with don't live around here.

"I pretty much lost contact with the moms from Sabrina's play groups. It's awkward when I run into them now. They're friendly enough, but without kids in common, the connection is lost."

She looked at Dan. "They've all changed. Not a single relationship is the same. Even Carrie looks at me strange some days, wondering when I'm going to break, I'm sure. She's always trying to get me back into counseling."

"So you tried it then," Dan asked. "Counseling?"

She nodded. "Yes, for a while. It helped a bit, gave me some coping mechanisms, and got me functioning in the world again, leaving the house. When you do the kind of work I do, and work from home there aren't a lot of reasons to get up and dressed some mornings. At a certain point the counselor pushed me to get used to life without Sabrina and move on. That will never happen, so I stopped making appointments."

"Can you think of anyone who stopped all contact with you, cut you right out of their life?"

"Pete and I don't see much of one another. You already know we were ready to separate when it happened. We just needed to figure out how to do it in a way that wouldn't tear our daughter's life apart. With Bree gone, we no longer had a reason to stay together, let alone stay in touch."

"How does he act when you do see him around town?"

"He's angry, blames me for what happened. We manage to be civil most days. I lost a few mutual friends in the divorce, but so did he. For the most part, we don't socialize in the same circles anymore. I see him maybe once or twice a month when we cross paths at the grocery store, or the gas station, places like that. We still share the same dentist. He likes the bar scene, Carrie's mentioned seeing him a time or two, but I never go to bars with her."

"Any other significant changes in your life?"

She gave him a pointed stare. "Finding Sabrina is my sole focus. I live a pretty solitary life, Dan. I check in with the police often to see about new leads. I go for breakfast every Saturday at Ruby's, hit the grocery store a couple times a week, pop into the library once in a while. Sometimes I even go to the movies with Carrie and the girls, but that's pretty much it. I've taken on a lot of contracts and buried myself in work."

"You're still doing graphic design?"

She nodded. "But I'd already decided to take a break when the visions started again. I'm one hundred percent devoted to this. What about you? Don't you have other cases?"

"I'm free to take on the cases I like. If it becomes necessary, the team will come down to back us up, but for now let's keep it to just you and me." A group of twenty-somethings crowded into the pub, bringing the noise of Friday night rush hour traffic with them.

23

"Looks like the evening crowd is starting to make its way in. Pretty soon we're going to need sign language to communicate. The food is excellent here. Why don't we order some to go and head up to the conference room at the office," Dan suggested. "You can fill me in on whatever else you think I should know. Then we can practice being a couple on the verge of a serious commitment." Dan grinned at the look of exasperation that crossed her face as she picked up the menu.

# Chapter Four

Rebecca stopped outside her home office. Dan's eyes drifted past where she stood, landing on the closed door at the other end of the hall. "I haven't changed a lot since you were last here, except for adding the sofa-bed. It's quite comfortable. I've slept on it a number of times."

He stared at Bree's door a moment longer before turning to look in Rebecca's spare room. She waited for him to ask why she slept in her office when she had a bedroom down the hall.

"This is fine," he murmured.

"The closet has space for your clothes and bag. I've moved my laptop to my room, so feel free to use the desk for your things." Rebecca hid a grimace when her hand shook as she pointed toward the next room. "You can use the bathroom in the hall. I have an ensuite in my bedroom." Christ, she sounded like she ran a bed and breakfast. Next, she'd be telling him when to appear for meals and filling him in on interesting things to see and do in the area.

"I'd like to work at the dining room table if that's okay with you," Dan said. "More room to spread out. If anyone comes by all they'll see is a person set up to work from home. Since you work upstairs, it's a natural place."

"Whatever works for you. People generally don't pop in here though. If someone's coming by I usually know ahead of time. I'm going to make some sandwiches. You hungry?"

Dan grinned. "I could eat." Rebecca remembered that about him. She didn't know how the man stayed so lean. He always seemed to be eating. Then again, his tight T-shirt revealed muscles everywhere and she read somewhere that muscles burned more calories.

"You set up while I make lunch." Rebecca headed for the stairs.

"I don't expect you to cook and clean for me. I know how to prepare a meal and make a bed."

She laughed. "Well, that's a relief. I'm not known for my culinary prowess. Salads, sandwiches, and stir fry are the usual fare around here. Some variety sounds nice."

"Why don't I take care of dinner then?" Dan offered.

"Might have to go grocery shopping first."

Dan pulled his laptop out of the bag, located an outlet, and placed his computer on the table nearby. "Perfect," he said. "Give people in town a chance to check me out and give me a feel for their reactions."

Rebecca tucked a strand of hair behind her ear. "Do you really think this will work?" she asked, more of herself than of Dan.

"I know it will." He placed some papers beside the laptop and angled his head toward the kitchen. "What about those sandwiches?"

Rebecca washed the lettuce with shaking hands and fought the longing for a glass of wine to settle her nerves. She needed to remain whole and functioning when Bree came home. And a clear head for when Dan asked to see Bree's room again.

He used to sit in there while he thought through the case, as though being closer to her helped him connect with the monster who took her. Rebecca wanted to remind him of that, and force him to examine why being surrounded by Bree's things heightened his focus. But he needed to get there on his own.

Something similar had to happen there today. Rebecca needed Bree's presence to surround Dan, for her light to fill him. If he planned to invest his soul in this, he must first feel her loss. He'd never feel the heartbreak as keenly as she did, Rebecca understood that, but his receptors needed to open before they'd be able to receive. The visions held the answers, but he didn't believe in them. Yet.

With the awkward lunch behind them, Rebecca worked to settle her nerves. Dan could only do so much to carry his end of the conversation.

"I'll clean this up. Why don't you go relax for a bit?" He paused. "If you don't mind, when I'm done here, I'd like to go up to Bree's room."

A shudder passed through her as she watched his hand raise and then lower to the table again, knowing his fingers itched to cover her own as he did so often in the past.

Color rode up her cheeks, she knew. Heat blazed from her neck across her face, and she cursed her pale Irish skin. "Yeah, I figured that. You spent so much time there before." Taking a deep breath she pushed the words out, astounded that the very thing she wanted was so hard to allow. Her chest ached at the thought of opening old wounds. "Give me a minute first."

"Sure." Dan lifted the dishes and headed into the kitchen while Rebecca went upstairs, timing her breathing with each step.

The door opened with reluctance.

Tones of sunny yellow spread throughout the room. Haystack on her walls because Bree loved the paint name. Curtains the color of sunrise because—Lord help her—Bree loved to get up early just to watch the sun peek over the horizon. A white and yellow daisy duvet draped over the bed. A collection of buttons, in every shade of yellow imaginable, sat in a mason jar on the white Victorian dresser, with a scrap of yellow and white gingham stretched over the lid.

The net hanging in the corner held Sabrina's menagerie of stuffed animals, most indistinguishable but for three clear favorites arranged just so with Winnie the Pooh snuggled in next to Simba, who rested beneath Stretch, the golden spotted giraffe, complete with bald patches crowning the pile.

Rebecca needed Dan to see this room again but at the same time feared it might reveal how fragile she'd become. On a good day Rebecca felt as ferocious as Simba hanging in the corner, but most days she fell apart. As soon as Dan walked in he'd see the truth. But she wasn't in this fight alone anymore. She had to learn to count on him to have her back and Sabrina's back too. However, trust had to flow both ways.

She wiped the lone tear away upon hearing Dan's footsteps on the stairs, sensed the heat of him at her back. His hands settled on her shoulders.

"You okay?"

Rebecca turned to see his reaction to the room, and felt, more than heard, him suck in his breath.

Dan walked around her, his eyes taking in the familiar tableau. He crouched down next to the overflowing laundry basket and picked up a T-shirt from the pile, lifting it to his nose. A deep sigh escaped him as he looked away.

Rebecca gnawed on her bottom lip, knowing he judged her, and hating that it bothered her so much.

"You haven't washed these, have you?" Dan asked, his voice gentle. He looked toward the bed. "You haven't washed the bedding either?"

She opened her mouth, but couldn't get the words past the lump in her throat.

Dan stood up and continued his tour, stopping now and then to pick up a toy, or stroke his finger along the curve of the dresser. When he picked up the jar of buttons, gave it a little shake and then put it down several inches over from where it sat before, Rebecca curled her fingers into fists, but kept her silence. At one point, she thought she caught a frown crossing his face, but he turned toward the window before she could be sure. He stood looking out for the longest time, his dark hair in sharp contrast to the pale yellow curtains.

When Dan finally turned, his eyes landed on the wine glass on the bedside table. A smear of red stained the bottom. He walked over, picked it up, and sniffed.

Damn, she didn't realize she left it there. Rebecca swallowed her shame, remembering what happened the last time they were in this room together, the day Dan left. No excuse justified their behavior. Not the two bottles of wine they shared, not the news that the rest of Dan's team were already packed up and gone, and certainly not her grief. Closing her eyes couldn't block the memory of the anger in that first kiss, or the desperation in what followed. Her lack of inhibition in those moments still tormented her, pushing her toward another drink every day since then.

Dan shook his head. He kept his expression neutral, but the clenched jaw gave him away.

"What are you doing here, Rebecca?" he kept his voice low and controlled.

Rebecca squared her shoulders and met his accusing stare. "Whatever it takes to get through each day without my daughter." She walked over and grabbed the glass from his hand. "This has nothing to do with anything. You're here to help me find Bree, not to judge me."

"Hiding your pain behind booze is a coping mechanism, one you've used since the day Sabrina disappeared. It didn't work then, and it won't work now. I can't help someone who won't help herself." Dan spun back to the window, but not before Rebecca saw disappointment and the shadow of guilt in his eyes.

"Damn you," Rebecca shouted. "You have no idea. You don't have a gaping hole in your heart, or wake up crying every night hugging a damn pillow instead of your child."

He looked at her and the pity on his face pushed her back to the wall.

"I have a few drinks now and again, so what. I'm human. Don't judge me for how I choose to grieve." She swiped her fingers over her wet face. "Don't judge where you've never been."

"Be honest here. Can you do this? Can you get past the rest of the crap and focus on getting your child back?" He looked around. "From what I'm seeing here, I'd say no."

Rebecca's back slid down the wall until she sat knees to chest. "Don't take this away from me. It's all I've got. I'm tired of feeling dead inside." She met his eyes while leaning her head back. "The drinking helped, for a while. When I realized I needed to be stronger for Bree, I stopped. I haven't been in this room since the day I came to see you in Phoenix. I'm stronger and part of that is because of you."

"I can't be the reason your world falls apart."

"What are you talking about?"

"Don't stop drinking for me, because when you fail it's one more strike against me."

"Everything I do is for Bree." She reached for his hand and tugged him down next to her on the floor. They sat side-by-side, legs out straight. "I'm grateful to have you to lean on, someone to help me navigate the clues. I won't ever," Rebecca lifted her head and turned to look at him, "*ever* blame you for what happens this time. I won't fall apart. I promise to tell you if something is too much for me to handle. But I need you to keep an open mind." She placed a finger over his mouth. "Don't say anything yet. Yes. I've been struggling a lot lately. At last, I have my head on straight and it feels good. God, my head is so clear it's scary. But I know I can backslide too. I'm strong, but not strong enough to fight you on this." His finger brushed the tear sliding down her cheek. "I need to know you don't think I'm crazy, that you'll help me find Bree. I want to trust you, and I can't afford to waste energy hiding things from you. "

Rebecca couldn't read him, couldn't tell which way he leaned. His lengthy silence made her wonder if he was going to answer at all. His voice startled her when he spoke.

"I'm not sure what your goal is here. You've lead me along some predetermined path, revealing the pieces that fit your agenda and not much else."

She leaned her head back against the wall, and hid behind closed eyes.

"I know, at the heart of things, you think what you're doing is justified. My feelings don't matter, not my real feelings. You only want me to feel what works for you. And you want to punish me a bit too, because I took what you offered, and then walked away from both you and Sabrina. I understand that.

"If this is going to work, then we need to be honest with each other. We had this conversation three years ago, but if you want to go another round, fine. I took advantage. I was unprofessional and insensitive and way out of line. I'm not proud of the way I behaved or how things ended. We've done the accusation and apology dance to death. I don't know what else to say. When you came to my office, I took it as a sign that you were past it, or at least willing to work around it. Was I wrong?"

Rebecca shook her head. He was right, of course. She should have known better then to think they could get through this day without rehashing their past. "I'm not looking for another apology. I take equal blame for what happened in a drunken moment of stupidity. Right now, I just want to find my daughter and I need your help to do it."

He stood up. "You've got my help. Just don't try to control me, or make me feel the same way you do. You don't want that. Not deep inside. And, don't think for a moment that I am not connected to Sabrina, that my heart isn't involved, because you're wrong. Let me know if you think we can make this work when you come downstairs."

Rebecca remained seated, staring down into the empty wine glass, wondering if she just turned her only ally against her.

# Chapter Five

"This is ridiculous," Rebecca muttered on the third day as she picked up a pair of jeans from the laundry basket and began folding them. She and Dan settled into a routine of sorts in the past few days, watching their words, and timing their room entries and exits based on each other's whereabouts. "Really ridiculous," she muttered again, pulling something white out of the pant leg and realizing she held a pair of Dan's briefs.

"What's ridiculous?" Dan asked on his way through the living room to the kitchen, empty coffee cup in hand. His feet changed direction when he saw the underwear in her hands. "I'm sorry. They must have been left behind in the dryer. It's nothing to get upset about. I'll take them." He tucked a corner of the underwear into his pocket and continued into the kitchen, white cotton bouncing against his backside with each step.

"I wasn't upset," Rebecca called after him, "and I wasn't talking about your underwear." She grumbled as she went back to folding and stacking the clothes on the sofa.

"What were you talking about then?" Rebecca spun around to find Dan sipping his coffee right behind her.

"Don't sneak up on me like that." Her hand went to her chest.

"Sorry." Dan grinned, unrepentant. His eyes twinkled as he stared at the scrap of black lace dangling from her fingertips.

She shoved the panties deep into the basket and picked up a T-shirt instead.

"Well?"

"Well what?" Rebecca placed the folded top on the pile and started folding the next one.

Dan raised one brow. "What were you going on about then, while you fondled my briefs?"

Rebecca rolled her eyes, refusing to let him bait her. "You, if you must know."

She reached for a pair of shorts, but Dan's hand on her forearm stopped her.

"What about me?"

Rebecca dropped the shorts back into the basket and faced him. "Why be stubborn and waste time over something that shouldn't even be an issue?"

Dan set his cup down on the coffee table and folded his arms across his chest.

"You think your drinking isn't an issue?"

"Not anymore."

"You got embarrassed when the cashier at the drug store smirked as she rang up our purchases."

"You bought condoms, for God's sake." Rebecca felt her cheeks flush. "I can imagine what Susan must have thought." She was disconcerted more by what that little item implied about Dan's intentions, than with Susan's reaction.

"She thought exactly what I wanted her to think," Dan said. "She spent the entire ten minutes we spent shopping gossiping on the phone with her friends. What better way to spread the word?"

Rebecca sighed.

"Aha. That's my point." Dan unfolded his arms and pointed at her. "You keep telling me you can handle what people think, along with the stress and tension. I'm not sure you can. Do you honestly feel able to cope with what we may find out there? It's not going to be pretty. It never is, especially where missing kids are involved."

"I'm in charge of how I feel. That's what adults do. If I can't deal, I'll tell you." She angled her head toward a yellow laundry basket in the corner, the one from Bree's room. "I'm not as fragile as you think."

"You washed Bree's clothes?" she heard the surprise in his voice.

Rebecca looked out the window before answering. "Not yet, no. But they're one floor closer to the laundry room and before the day is over they'll go in the washer."

"That's a good start." Dan looked impressed.

"It's a damn good start and you know it." She walked to the basket and nudged it with her toe. "I know they're just Bree's things, not her. I also know Bree is coming back to me." Rebecca picked up the same top Dan held in Bree's room. The room swayed, even as the pain attacked her temples. Gasping, Rebecca reached toward Dan.

"What is it? What's wrong?" He picked her up and carried her to the sofa, shoving the pile of folded clothes to the floor. "Talk to me, Rebecca. Come on, tell me what's happening." Her mouth opened and her eyes rolled back in her head. She started shivering, convulsing almost. Dan pulled his cellphone from his back pocket. "I'm calling 911, Rebecca, hold on."

"No," she forced out. "I'll be okay. It'll pass soon. Just stay with me," she whispered, her hands went to her temples, and her head rocked back and forth.

She turned onto her side and curled up in a fetal position, moaning. "No bloody way," Dan rasped.

"Please don't," she gripped his hand. "Please."

Dan stared at her, relenting when her shaking subsided. "Okay." He set his phone beside him on the coffee table. He sat on the end of the couch and lifted her head, gently placing it on his lap. "But if things change, I'm calling."

With his left arm trapped under her neck, he wrapped the other around her and reached for her hand. Then, he watched and waited.

Surrounded by Dan's strength, Rebecca released herself to the vision.

*A blurry mass of red clay loomed before her. One of the mountains in the park? Which one? The image cleared, revealing more details. Red clouds of dust rose beneath each booted footfall of those walking ahead of her. She saw outlines of two people, but sensed more ahead of them. It was night but the path seemed well lit. She looked up. A full moon hovered overhead. The path became steeper, harder to navigate. The skittering cascading pebbles and stones reached her, followed by a heavy thud.*

*"Here," a voice said, and then the clang of metal banging together. "Quickly, but make sure it's deep enough."*

*A bright light shone in her eyes and she recoiled. Flashlights. She could see the shovels now and three figures digging. One cloaked figure stood to the side, next to a Jumping Cholla. Two light colored canvas duffel bags, maybe three feet long, sat at his feet. One was empty the other bulged. Could that have been the thud she heard, someone*

33

*dropping the bags?*

*Her eyes were drawn back to the tree. Something about it seemed off. Larger than normal, she realized, with a strange shape.*

*Goosebumps covered her arms and gusts of wind pushed at her. Flying dirt swirled amid the flowing robes before falling to the ground. It had to be below fifty degrees, unheard of for August, even up here.*

*"That's enough," said the voice, "throw the bag in." The tallest of the diggers tossed the bag in the hole with minimum effort. "Cover it up, and make it quick. I need to be back within the hour."*

Rebecca's eyelids fluttered then opened wide to stare into Dan's worried face.

"Thank God," he whispered. "Are you okay?"

Rebecca's hand flew to her mouth and covered it. A universal symbol Dan immediately understood. He rose up with Rebecca in his arms and headed to the main floor powder room.

"I can manage." She swallowed twice, fighting the urge. "Leave me alone for a minute."

"Not on your life." He gathered her auburn curls and pulled them away from her face as she leaned over and heaved. Dan's large hand stroked her hair when she sat back on her heels. "Done?"

At her shaky nod, his hand cupped her elbow helping her to stand. He rubbed his face with his free hand. "Jesus, Rebecca, what the hell just happened?"

"Let me clean up first then I'll explain as much as I can." Rebecca leaned against the vanity while Dan brought her a cup and her toothbrush and paste. Her strength slowly returned. "How long was I out?" she asked as Dan helped her back to the sofa.

He got her settled, then looked at his watch as he sat in the chair opposite her. "Twenty minutes maybe, I'm not sure. Definitely not more. I poured my coffee around nine. It's almost nine thirty now." He leaned forward and rested his elbows on his knees, fingers laced together. "You want to explain this, Rebecca?"

"Not really, but I will." She curled her legs under her. "I could use a glass of tea though." Dan got it for her then resumed his position.

"All right, enough stalling. Spill it."

"I think you know what happened." Stubborn silence stared her down. "A vision happened." She looked at him and cocked her head to the side. "I've never had anyone witness one before. I'm curious about what happens when I'm out."

"Yeah, well I'm not quite up to reliving it at the moment. You never let on that your episodes were this violent." Dan reached for his now cold coffee, grimaced at the taste, but drank it anyway before putting the empty mug down.

"They aren't really." Her stomach did a little flip when he raised one eyebrow. "Not as a rule." He stared at her. "It's only recently they became so intense," she admitted. "Someone's really trying to get my attention."

Dan's head dropped to rest on in his hands. "Christ Rebecca, you took ten years off my life with that stunt. Shouldn't you see a doctor?"

Her expression softened. "I'm fine," she said, raising her glass of tea. "Once I get my blood sugar up again I'll be back to myself. This part is normal." He continued to look doubtful.

"You're calling this a vision. Have you considered it a stress induced nightmare?"

"Is that what you think, after what you just witnessed?" Doubt crept into his eyes, just a shadow around the edges, but there all the same.

"Can you pinpoint what made it different?"

"I'm not sure how long I'm usually out for, but I tend to only get snippets or flashes. This one played like a scene in a movie." She tapped her nails on the side of the glass. "I'd like to know what happens when I have a vision, from your point of view."

"That can wait. Tell me the details while they're still fresh. No wait a minute." He grabbed a pad of paper and a pen from the dining room table and sat back down.

Rebecca went through it from beginning to end, while Dan asked the occasional question and took notes.

"You saw four people then? All men?"

"I think so. I only heard one voice, male for sure. The other three were big, so I took them as men."

"Did you see their faces?"

"The robes had hoods." She suddenly remembered. "And they all wore them up over their heads."

"Good, any other details you can remember about the robes?"

"They were dark colored."

"Did you get an impression of what might be in the second bag? You said only one digger tossed it in the hole?"

"That's right, and he did it one handed, so it can't have weighed much. A round shape filled one end, like a bowling ball…" Rebecca's voice trailed off as her eyes filled with horror. "Oh my God—or a small body."

"Don't jump to conclusions." Dan tried to reassure her, his expression grim.

"It could have been a child," she gasped. "Bree?" Dan rounded the table, lifted her up and sat her back down on his lap. One hand rubbed her back while the other wiped her tears.

"Calm down and think this through. You told me you saw Bree alive and older. If that were the case, and that's a big if, it's more likely to be someone else, Nicole Wilson maybe."

"You're right." Her breath shuddered out of her. She rubbed her temples.

"Could you tell where this happened? Which peak?" His hand continued stroking her back.

Rebecca thought for a minute. "I'm just not sure; I can't get a clear picture."

Dan set her aside, tore a page from his book, and then handed her the page and his pen. "Draw it for me."

"I'm a terrible artist."

"Doesn't matter. Just get whatever comes to mind down on paper."

Rebecca sketched the peak, twisting paths, rocks, pebbles, and the oddly shaped Jumping Cholla. Then stared at it. "Nothing. It doesn't look familiar at all. I know the area well, I grew up here, but it's a big park, and I don't know every peak by site. It could be anywhere."

Rebecca handed the picture to him. She caught herself admiring his form, back lit by the sun pouring in through the window behind him. Nice, she thought. He raised the picture higher, concentrating on the detail at the bottom.

As he held the page up, the sun streamed through the paper, causing it to become transparent revealing the reverse image.

She jumped up and tore the page out of his hands, holding it backwards up to the light. "Oh my God, I know this spot."

"Are you sure?"

"Yes, yes I'm sure. This is the anteater. Well, a cacti shaped like one," she said, smiling at his raised brows. "I can't believe I didn't see it at first." She turned to him, showing him how she flipped around the paper. Carrie and I climbed here all the time." She looked back at the drawing. "It's been years, but I recognize this. Wait, I have a picture." She ran to the sideboard in the dining room and pulled out a photo album. She handed it to him and grabbed a book off the coffee table, flipping through its pages.

"Here." She handed Dan the book open to page twenty-nine, took the photo album back, and flipped to a page close to the beginning. She pumped her fist in the air. "Yes, I knew I still had it." She placed the photo of Carrie and her beside the picture in the book Dan held.

He frowned. "If you say so..."

Rebecca flipped over the sketch she drew. "Here, hold this up to the light for me," she said, then lifted the photo album next to it and smiled at Dan's reaction.

He smiled and traced his fingers along the red ponytail of one of the girls in the picture, each holding rabbit ears behind the other's head. "You?"

She pointed to the blond teenager. "And this is Carrie. We were seventeen. I got a camera for my birthday that year and went snap happy. It had a timer so we'd set it on a rock and take pictures of ourselves. See that?" Rebecca pointed to the Jumping Cholla in the background. "See? An anteater. This is it, I know it."

"It matches."

She leaned in and put her arms around him, before pulling back with a big smile. Dan brought his hands up to her back when she hugged him and used them now to move her closer until her firm breasts pressed against his chest. Her smile faded. Her tongue slipped out to moisten dry lips.

Dan caught the movement before lifting his gaze to meet hers. A muffled curse filled the air before he leaned down slowly meeting her lips, dragging a low moan from Rebecca. He sank into the kiss, parting

37

her lips and delving inside when she opened to him. Sparks flared low in her abdomen.

As if he knew desire ricocheted inside her, Dan lowered his hands to her hips and pressed her against him. Flames of heat licked at her, dipping lower, and wetness pooled between her thighs when she encountered the hard ridge behind the front of his jeans. Her knees buckled, and her arms tightened around his neck, a whimper escaping this time.

# Chapter Six

Dan caught her, pressed her even closer, before he pulled his lips away and took a step back.

Rebecca watched him struggle to bring his breathing under control and pressed a hand to her stomach. A guilty thrill moved through her when his fingers brushed over her lips, until his face hardened, and he dropped his hand.

"I'm sorry. We agreed we weren't going to do this."

Rebecca looked away. They had. She just needed to get her traitorous body on the same page. One kiss and every sweaty detail of that night came back to tempt her.

He turned and headed toward the kitchen, picking up his mug and her glass on the way. "Tell me more about the area in the picture. Is it possible for us to get there today?" He placed the mugs in the sink, keeping his back to her.

"It's doable in half a day, but August is a bad month for hiking. Even if we left now we'd be there during the hottest part of the day."

"What if we don't do the full loop? We can backtrack once we've found the spot we're looking for." He faced her. "Can you handle it?"

She got the impression his question dealt with more than an afternoon hike. She swallowed. "I've hiked those trails in all kinds of weather. We'll need to be prepared. If we throw some gear together, bring something to eat, and lots of water, we can do it."

"How's the access once the road ends, I can't see them carrying the bags any great distance."

"No cars. Search and Rescue uses ATV's and serious off-road vehicles. The hike gets steep in places. If it's the spot I'm thinking of, we'll be hiking about forty minutes in."

"Good. Let's get some things together then."

"We can stop by Ruby's since it's on the way," Rebecca suggested. "And order some food to go."

They pulled into Ruby's fifteen minutes later, a case of water and a couple of backpacks piled on the back seat. Josh frowned when he opened the door for them on his way in. "Morning, Rebecca." He gave her a warm smile, and Dan a quick nod. "I'm not used to seeing you in town on a weekday. How are things?"

Rebecca smiled back. "Just fine, thanks for asking. You here for your morning coffee break?"

"I need some extra caffeine to keep me going these days." He looked at his watch and winced. "I don't have much time left so I'd best see Ruby. See you on Saturday, Rebecca." Josh headed over to the counter.

Dan glanced at Rebecca. "You two have a date?"

Rebecca laughed. "A date? With Josh? I eat here every Saturday. Josh is one of the other regulars."

"He's got it bad for you." Dan's smile widened when her head swung in Joshua's direction.

"You're imagining things. Besides, he's just a kid."

"A kid with feelings for you. Put him out of his misery if you're not planning on returning his feelings."

"Your Spidey sense is off. He's just a kid with good manners. A crush?" Rebecca shook her head and laughed as she caught Ruby's eye.

Ruby waved them on to a table near the back. "I've got the order you called in almost ready. Take a seat there for a few while I pack it up."

Ruby disappeared into the back room and returned to hand Josh his coffee and a small paper bag.

"How long will it take to get to Red Eye?" Dan asked. "And who's that old man over by the window staring holes in me?"

Rebecca leaned over to see around Dan, then smiled and waved. "That's Jim Grimly, the town pessimist. He always has that look. The drive's about twenty-five minutes," she continued, "give or take. Serious hikers won't be out today. It's too hot. The foolish and ignorant will head out, but I doubt they'll attempt the trickier trails. Red Eye's ranked as difficult in the guides. My guess is we'll have the trail to ourselves."

"Did I hear you mention Red Eye?" Ruby asked, setting a large sack to-go on the table. "It's a little late in the day to start that trek, isn't it?"

"Can you believe Dan's lived in the area for almost six years and has never hiked the trails? He's a tenderfoot so I'm not planning on doing the full loop. I just want to give him a taste." Rebecca peeked in the bag. "The food smells delicious, as usual. Thanks." Rebecca looked at Dan. "You ready?"

Dan put on a reluctant face to go along with Rebecca's story, and then smiled at Ruby. "I hope she knows what she's doing."

"Don't you worry." Ruby patted his arm. "There's no one better than our girl here to guide you. Take care now," she said, already heading back behind the counter. Dan opened the door for Rebecca and held it there while the next customer came in. He looked around to say goodbye to Ruby, but when he saw her pick up the phone, he sent her a wave and a smile instead.

"Busy place," he said to Rebecca.

She smiled and held the bag up. "Good food."

Dan headed east on Route 60 for a stretch, before turning left onto Red Eye Road. A few other cars were parked at the pay station when they got there. Dan made quick work of transferring the food and water into their packs. "Lead the way," he said, shrugging his pack into place.

The difficult trail challenged experienced hikers, which didn't come close to describing Dan's level of expertise. Rocks turned underfoot with each step, making Rebecca grateful they both wore hiking boots. Rivulets of sweat ran down her back, and Dan's shirt looked soaked.

"Any other hikers will be well ahead of us, given how late we started out." Rebecca stepped around a large boulder.

They hiked for close to an hour before Rebecca veered left off the trail and headed up a steep embankment. She looked back at Dan, anticipating his question.

"They came this way; I recognize that Cactus over there, the one that looks like an anteater." Rebecca saw the Jumping Cholla from her picture, a much older and larger specimen now. "There." She pointed to the left. "Just over that rise."

A loud crack rent the air. Rebecca cried out and went down, a cloud of dust rose a foot from where she lay.

"Stay down," Dan yelled. He swung the backpack around and reached for the gun in the front pocket, and then threw himself down beside her. "Are you hit?"

"No, I just twisted my ankle on a rock. My ego took a hit, but I'm fine otherwise." The weight of Dan's arm stopped her when she started to rise. "What's going on?"

Dan edged her closer to the dense bush beside them. A saguaro cactus blocked them from the other side. "Someone just took a shot at us."

"With a gun?"

"Yes, with a gun. Good thing I brought my own." Rebecca's eyes widened at the sight of the gun in his hand. She knew agents carried guns, but never saw Dan with his drawn.

"They can't be shooting at us. They must have seen a snake."

"That bullet landed a foot from you and there's no one around us. Unless someone's worried about a snake twenty yards away from them, they were aiming for one of us."

Dan inched his head above the brush and scanned the area. "I don't see him, but he's out there." Another crack sounded, and a green chunk of flesh flew off the cactus next to them.

"Shit." Dan's hand rammed her head into the dirt. "Keep your head down."

He spider crawled a few feet away, using the dense plant life as cover. He rose to his knees and fired off three quick shots in the direction of a cluster of cacti about thirty feet away. He advanced, chasing the gunman back along the path they just traveled, stopping at the top of the rise. The sound of hoof beats drowned out the harsh breaths Rebecca hadn't even been aware of taking. Dan followed the cloud of dust, disappearing from sight, and then walked back to where Rebecca waited. His curses reached her long before he did.

"He's on horseback, headed away from us. There's no way I'm catching up to him. We'll lay low here a bit longer, just to be sure." He helped her to a sitting position. "You okay? How's the ankle?"

Rebecca circled it around. "It's all right. I'll be fine to walk out of here." She looked over her shoulder, then at Dan. "We're so close, seems a shame to give up."

Dan looked back to the trail of dust fading in the distance and nodded his head. "He won't be sneaking up on me a second time." He held his gun as they walked the few yards to the spot Rebecca remembered. The ground leveled out and offered a decent vantage point. Dan studied the area. He nodded toward where their shooter holed up and glanced over the spot where Rebecca went down before the ground sloped down again. There was nothing else in the way of cover.

"It doesn't look like anything's been buried here recently. The night air held a chill in my vision. It must have been during winter."

"Can you point out the exact spot?" he asked, keeping his eyes on the surrounding area.

Rebecca circled the area then stood five feet from the Jumping Cholla. "Here." She pointed to a spot three feet away. "And the fourth man stood there."

Dan walked over and handed her the gun, giving her a quick lesson in how to use it. "If anything moves out there, shoot it." He unzipped his backpack, took out a folding shovel, and started digging.

Rebecca kept vigil, passing her water bottle to Dan occasionally to keep him hydrated. The mid-day sun sucked fluids from them faster than they could replace them. The repetitive crunch of the shovel hitting dirt, followed by a swoosh as dirt slid onto the growing mound took Rebecca back to her vision, and she shivered at the memory. The soft thud of the shovel connecting with something solid dragged Rebecca's gaze back to Dan.

He sat back on his heels and returned her look, eyes wide. "Well, I'll be damned. It's a cream canvas tote bag." He waved her back as she started to get up. "No, you don't need to see this, and we don't want to contaminate the scene any more than we already have." An unmistakable stench rose up from the hole, and his hand rose up to his nose. He sighed. "I'm going to have a hard time explaining this to the authorities as it is."

Reaching into the backpack, he pulled out a pair of latex gloves and put them on.

"I just want to be sure what's in there before I bring them in. These men could have been dumping anything." He straddled the hole and reached down. Rebecca heard a rustle of cloth and the muted sound of a zipper and saw Dan turn his face from her. "Damn it."

"You don't have to say it. I know it's a child."

Dan came over and crouched down. "It's a body," he corrected.

"We won't know for sure if it's a child until Forensics arrives." He tore off the gloves, and crammed them into a backpack. Then he swung both their packs over his shoulder and reached for her hand. "Come on." He tugged at her arm. "Let's find somewhere we can get phone reception."

He picked up a signal on the main path allowing Dan to call it in. They remained there, as instructed by the officer on the phone.

Dan spent most of the forty-minute wait pacing. Anger rolled off him in waves with each pass. She wanted Dan to care, Rebecca reminded herself. Only it wasn't so cut and dried anymore. Her feelings for Dan deepened with each day.

Dan made the next pass, stopped, opened his mouth as if to speak, and then went back to pacing without saying a word.

"Talk to me," Rebecca reached out to touch his arm. He recoiled. Finding irrefutable evidence that proved her visions existed, painted her as a freak in his eyes, she knew it. Now he couldn't stand to be near her, never mind her touching him. Her eyes misted over and she turned away. Rebecca swung back again, angry with herself. She couldn't get anything past the lump on the first try and cleared her throat to try again.

She poked him in the chest. "Most people can't handle what I can do, which is why I don't go around advertising it. I thought you would be different. Kinder, at least." She stared him down.

"What are you talking about?"

"You're treating me like I have an infectious disease."

"What? What makes you think that?"

"Maybe because you can't stand to look at me, never mind touch me. And you haven't said ten words to me in the last twenty minutes."

"I'm just thinking, Rebecca." He rubbed his hands over his face. "And trying to figure out how I'm going to explain this to the police." He dropped his hands. "I wasn't thinking about how that would look to you. I take it you've had a few extreme reactions when you tell people about your visions."

"You could say that."

"I apologize. It's no excuse, but I'm also mad as hell the bastard got as close as he did without my noticing him." He looked away. "To be honest, until I saw that rotting bag in the ground, I still doubted your vision." He took a step closer. "I'm most of the way there, but not all.

And my overconfidence nearly got you killed." His fingers wove through her hair when he framed her face with his hands. "If anything had happened to you—"

"It's okay. I might have overreacted a tad." She gave him a rueful smile. "I get a bit defensive sometimes. This isn't your fault. It isn't even your fight."

Before she could stop herself, Rebecca rose up on her toes and kissed him. Her lips pressed softly at first, traveling over his cheeks, his brow and his eyelids before returning to his lips. At that point, he took control of the kiss. He ground his lips against hers and thrust his tongue inside, while sliding his hands over her shoulders and pressing her closer. A current of desire shot through her. Her breasts swelled and her womb contracted.

She ran her hands around his back, holding him close. Dan pulled his lips from hers with a gasp, and buried his lips in her neck, drawing a deep moan from her. One of his hands came between them, heading toward her breast, circling in but stopping short of the aching peak at the center.

Rebecca shifted and trembled when his thumb slid over her sensitive nipple. Frantically, she raised her hands and brought his head back up, needing to taste him again.

They jumped apart at the sound of voices on the path.

\* \* \* \*

Rebecca's anxiety heightened with each step. Dan put off the Deputy Sheriff's questions where the trail made talking difficult, but the time for explanations neared. Dammit, she went to great lengths to hide her visions all these years. Dan knew. She told him during the initial investigation, but due to his disbelief, Rebecca doubted he filled in the rest of the team. Even if he did, they never told anyone in town, or she'd know about it by now.

There'd be no keeping this quiet. The press would jump on it and not just the locals either.

Rebecca thought back to the day the police officer had come to their door all those years ago. She should have been in bed like a good little five year-old, but something woke her. Not the officers at the door, she remembered standing in the hall when their knock came. It was her mother's voice calling to her. She stubbed her bare toe on the chipped baseboard in her haste to find her mother and give her a kiss goodnight, and cried out when she saw the officer talking to daddy instead. "Something bad happened to mommy," she told her father. "She isn't coming home."

Her father discovered her secret that day, and everything changed. "Baby. You can never tell anyone about these dreams you have, okay?" he cried, when she told him later how she knew. His entire body trembled. His fingers bit into her shoulders and gave her a hard shake. "No one. Do you understand baby-girl? Promise me." Another quick shake and she nodded her head, tears streaming down her face.

"I p-p-promise, da-daddy."

He gathered her into his arms and carried her to the sofa in the living room. He picked up Gerome the Giraffe and handed him to her as he sat down, gently placing her in his lap. She woke on the sofa the next morning, snuggled under her mother's favorite afghan, to the sound of soft voices in the kitchen. Aunt Meg cried, tears dripping into her coffee cup. When her father committed suicide six months later, Aunt Meg came, swooped her up in a big cushy hug, told her everything would be all right, and took her home. Rebecca never told Aunt Meg, or anyone else, about her visions until the day she told Dan.

She let out a sigh as they crested the small incline. Fate was about to flaunt her secrets for all to see.

Deputy Tate spoke quietly to his team before heading over to where Rebecca waited. Dan stood several meters away talking to another officer.

"I'm going to need your statement and an explanation of exactly what went on here today. One of my men will speak with you once we get things under control. He nodded at the officer standing by her left elbow and turned, already striding toward the small crowd gathered around the body. Rebecca looked to where Dan stood giving his statement, wishing she could talk with him again.

"Ms. McKenney? I'm ready to take your statement now." Rebecca jerked her head back to the officer standing guard over her.

He flipped his black notebook open and poised his pen over the page, ready to record her story and shatter the illusion of safety she spent two decades building.

He kept his expression neutral, a true professional, barely raising a brow, or pausing as she recited events. She watched his pen glide across the page, saw the life she created flow out of it. After what seemed like hours, they stopped, and someone handed her a bottle of water.

Rebecca looked around and found Dan chatting with Chief Bains and Deputy Tate. Their three heads bobbed as they spoke. She almost smiled; convinced law enforcement had a secret form of communication based on the art of the nod. The men all shook hands before Dan and Bains broke away and walked in her direction.

"You okay?" Dan gave Rebecca's arm a light squeeze while Bains spoke to the officer taking her statement.

Rebecca pulled away and rubbed her hands over her arms with a grimace. The night air chilled her after the intense heat of the day. "My statement went more like an interrogation, just like when Bree disappeared." She shook her head. "They won't believe the location of that body came to me in a vision. I'm pretty sure I'm suspect number one right now." She angled her chin to his right. "When did Chief Bains get here? This doesn't fall under his jurisdiction, does it?"

He smiled. "Let's call it inter-departmental cooperation. Bains has enough of a connection to you and Bree's case to convince Tate he can be of assistance. Tate's a good man, willing to accept help when offered. Funding cutbacks are affecting every department."

"I'm sure your FBI connection has a lot to do with his willingness to cooperate."

"It didn't hurt. Bains is waving us over. I think that's our ticket out of here."

Bains did the nod and shake thing again, then caught up to them. "You're both free to go for now, but be available for further questioning and don't leave town. I'll escort you to your vehicle."

Rebecca glanced at her watch, squinting to make out the numbers. She looked around, noticing how dark the area had become. The thought of hiking back to the car in the dark made her grimace. A grateful sigh escaped when Bains gestured to his off-road truck at the base of the incline. The emergency responder vehicles in these parts came well equipped for this terrain. They had to, especially Search and Rescue.

"Let's go." When Dan and Rebecca both climbed into the back seat, Bains shook his head but said nothing. Exhaustion made the drive back to the pay station a quiet one.

Bains parked next to Dan's car and leaned an elbow on the open window of the truck. "I'll need you to come to the station in the next day or so to go over your statements," he peered at Rebecca, "and see if there's anything you might like to change about them. I'll give you a call when I'm ready." He shifted gears, and then looked back at them. "I'd appreciate it if the two of you could try to stay out of trouble in the meantime." With another nod, he pulled away.

# Chapter Seven

Dan tossed his keys on the console in the front hall and walked over to his laptop.

"You're going to work on this now?" Rebecca glanced at her watch. "It's pretty late."

"I'll be up for a while anyway, processing the day."

"I don't think I'll sleep much either, to be truthful." Rebecca sat on the arm of the sofa, facing him. "Do you think Tate believed us?"

"Hard to say at this point. I think Chief Bains will have plenty of questions for us when he calls us in." Dan sat in the chair opposite her. "It's a lot for him to take in. A dead body doesn't show up every day in Cutter's Gulch." He smiled at her. "And I'm pretty sure psychics don't either. He'll come around. He'll consider the possibility that we knew the location of the body because we were involved. But what purpose would it serve for us to lead them straight to it?

"Bains will figure it out soon enough. It might take a while for him to come up with an alternate theory, but he's a smart cop. He'll follow the evidence."

"And where will that evidence lead?"

"With any luck, to the bastard who took a shot at us today. I'm convinced we're looking at one person. Either he's a terrible shot, or he only wanted to warn us off. In any case, it looks like someone didn't want us to find that body."

"And the fact that we have," Rebecca said as she stood and started pacing, "means we're on the right track."

"We've spooked him. He'll keep a close eye on us, and if we even hint at a new lead, he won't be firing warning shots." Dan snagged her hand on her next pass, standing to intercept her. "I made a mistake today. I left an opening, and someone got close to you. I won't let it happen again."

"Oh for God's sake. How could you have known? We were the only ones who knew about my vision." She pulled her hand away. "Unless someone is following me, no one knew where we were going."

"Ruby knew. We told her. So did anyone else in that diner today who might have been listening. And it's not beyond the realm of possibility that someone's keeping tabs on you. It's what I would do. We designed my sudden appearance here to arouse suspicion, and it worked. Damn it. I should not have been caught off guard today."

Dan pulled her in for a hug and tried to let his anger drain off. He rubbed his hands up and down her back to counteract the chill seeping through her body into his. He pulled back, just enough to frame her face with his hands. "I've been caught off guard in a number of ways today." The green in her eyes deepened. "This isn't supposed to happen."

"And yet, here we are."

"It complicates things."

"It doesn't have to. I'm no longer married, and I think I've proven I'm not about to fall apart at the first sign of trouble. We're two consenting adults. And we haven't had a single drink between us."

He leaned in for a taste, a quick nibble meant to appease the ache coursing through him. Memories of their one night together, never far from the surface, flared, overshadowing his intended objections. "There'll be no going back after this. If you're not sure, tell me now."

Rebecca reached down and rubbed her fingers over the bulge between them, smiling when Dan sucked in a breath, before covering her mouth with his. His hands slid to her hips, lifting her until her legs curled around his waist. She wound both arms around his neck as he headed for the stairs never parting his lips from hers.

He made it to the first landing before stopping to press her back to the wall and push himself against her heat with a deep groan.

Her hands headed for the button of his pants, but were knocked aside when he lifted her T-shirt up over her head, then flung it away. His fingers worked at the clasp of her bra and it sailed over the railing.

"Upstairs, hurry." Rebecca pushed his shirt up as far as it would go, their gasps mingling when her bare breasts pressed against the crisp hairs on his chest.

Dan shifted her up before cupping her butt and resuming the climb. He stopped once more outside the door to her room, his breathing ragged. His clouded eyes stared into hers. "Last chance, Becca, I don't want any regrets."

She finally managed the button on his pants with one hand, while holding on with the other. She leaned back, letting his arms hold her weight, and slid his zipper down. She reached in to stroke his heat. "No regrets," she whispered.

He carried her into the room and lowered her to the bed, following her down. She pushed against his chest and yanked his T-shirt off.

"Finally," she whispered against his skin, before leaving a trail of moist kisses across his chest. Her nails scraped his nipples, drawing his attention away from the throbbing pulse in her throat. He dealt with the rest of their clothes. He hugged her, and then rolled until she lay over him, breasts against his chest. Running his hands along the curve of her back, over the flare of her hips, he pressed until every inch of their bodies met, skin to skin, leaving room for nothing but the sweat of desire between them.

When she arched back, he palmed her breasts, pushing and squeezing, until they spilled over the tops of his fingers. The contrast of her pale skin against his tanned fingers fascinated him. Wanting to explore, he rolled them again, and bent his head to lick her midriff, her ribcage, and then the crease below her right breast, before honing in on the nipple standing up, begging for attention. He flicked it twice with his tongue, blew on it, and then watched it twitch in response before taking it into his mouth.

Her hands roamed over his hip and along his thighs. She pushed up to rub against his erection. Her nails clawed into his butt when he shifted to trail a hand down her body. His fingers drew a pattern on her abdomen and her inner thighs, before moving on to play in the dense tangle of curls.

Reaching down, Rebecca gripped his wrist to direct his hand, sighing at the iron strength of his forearms that resisted her efforts. He chuckled and eased her disappointment by transferring his mouth to her other breast. His fingers continued to dance around their target, every now and then, brushing oh so close, before drifting away again.

Rebecca pushed until he lay under her again. Smokey eyes taunted him, roaming over his body, widening at the impressive evidence of his need for her. She dipped her head and let her hair trail over his skin, weaving back and forth, caressing him from head to toe.

51

Dan wove his fingers through her wavy hair, content to let her decide her path. She paused over his erection, smiled when his length jerked and rose to play in the waves, and ignored his groan of complaint when she left that playground in search of another. She followed the path of his hair with her lips, trailed kisses over his abdomen as she worked her way up to his nipples, laving them with her soft tongue, like a cat lapping cream.

"Come back here," he growled and pulled her mouth up to meet his. He took his time, getting to know every crevice, lingering to duel with her tongue before sliding toward that spot in her neck; the one he knew made her knees buckle. He smiled at her groan.

Rebecca gasped as he slid his fingers between her folds without warning and found her slick with need. He caressed and tormented before finding her nub and pinching gently. She raised her hips, luring him deeper.

Rebecca's pupils dilated when he pushed two fingers deep inside her tight passage then stopped, waiting for her to adjust to him. Her wetness coated him. He worked her until her walls convulsed around his fingers and a scream of release slipped past her lips.

Panting, she reached for him, guiding him to her. Dan pulled back and fumbled for the pants on the floor. He pulled a condom from the pocket and slipped it on.

He looked down at Rebecca and rubbed the backs of his fingers across her abdomen. Her rosy skin flushed with her release. Still sensitive, her belly quivered, not quite finished. Her hands reached around his penis and squeezed before sliding rhythmically up and down.

His tongue reached out to intercept the bead of sweat rolling across her ribs. Rebecca's hands moved to his hair as his mouth continued downward, all pretense of play over. Spreading her thighs wide with his shoulders, he pressed his lips against her and closed his mouth over her, causing Rebecca to writhe beneath him.

"Inside me, now," she demanded. Her hands tugged at his hair. He rose up and settled his hips between her thighs.

Watching her closely, he slid his length into her. Rebecca accepted him easily. Covering her mouth with his, Dan began moving. Whimpers escaped her as she neared climax again, and she wrapped her legs around him while digging her heels in.

Dan moved faster, driving deep, then pulling out to plunge again. His lips ripped from hers, needing oxygen as he pumped, grunting as he closed in on the reward. With one final thrust, he pushed inside, straining before collapsing on top of her.

Her walls rippled around him, drawing the last of his reserves.

Panting, he raised her arms above her head and linked his fingers with hers. He pressed a gentle kiss to her neck; then covered her mouth with his. She smiled against his lips when he stirred inside her and shimmied her hips, eliciting a groan from him.

"Are you trying to kill me?"

"God, no," she exclaimed. "If I did, we wouldn't be able to do that again and I hope to do that many, many times."

He stirred again. "And then some."

He pulled out of her with a regretful sigh and rolled away to take care of the condom. He lay down on his left side again, aligning her body with his. "I like the way your body fits mine," he said. *Still,* he wanted to add, running his hand back and forth from hip to ribcage and sometimes further up, his thumb brushing against the side of her breast.

"I love the way you fit me too." The day finally caught up to Rebecca and a big yawn escaped her. She laughed, tilting her head to look at him. "Don't take it personally."

He smiled and pulled her closer, setting one of his legs between hers. He turned his head toward the window, hoping this wasn't the mistake he feared, and ran his fingers through the long strands of her hair. He leaned in to place a kiss on her temple when something caught his eye. He parted her hair and looked closer. What an odd place for a tattoo, he thought, drawing the sheet up over them. He'd have to ask her about it later.

# Chapter Eight

Dan pulled into the station lot just before seven thirty, five minutes earlier than he'd promised Chief Bains. "Other than his request that we get here as soon as possible so he can get this damned day over with, Bains said very little. They were able to ID the body, but nothing more. I couldn't get a feel for whether or not he planned to share anything else. I'm hoping to get a better read of him face to face. He'll likely have more questions for us too. Answer them truthfully and you'll be fine." He reached over and gave Rebecca's cold hand a squeeze. "You ready for this?" At her nod, he opened his door.

"There he is." Dan pointed across the street to the front door of Ruby's where Chief Bains stood, Styrofoam cup in hand. Bains waved, waiting for traffic to pass before he crossed to meet them.

Out of the corner of his eye, Dan caught a glimpse of a large shadow, advancing fast. His head swiveled toward Bains.

"Watch out!" he warned, shoving Rebecca to the ground and diving after her. All three turned at the squeal of tires. A large SUV, its lights off, bore down on Bains who'd almost reached them. They heard the violent thud of impact, and then the squeal of tires pulling away. Dan knelt next to where Rebecca lay on the ground, running his hands over her to assess the damage.

"I'm okay," she cried, her eyes glued to the figure lying in the road. "Check on the chief."

Dan ran over and put a hand on the chief's chest, holding him down when he began to rise. "You know the drill, Bains, stay here until the paramedics arrive." Officers poured out of the station and rushed to the street, while pedestrians stopped and stared.

"They've been called," an officer said, kneeling down beside the Chief. "What the hell happened out here?" he looked at Dan for answers.

"Some crazy ass driver ran me down," Bains interrupted, "and I'm capable of answering your questions myself Turner." Bains winced. "Damn fool broke my arm."

Dan looked around to see other officers securing the scene and

54

dealing with witnesses.

Bains turned his head toward Dan. "I couldn't catch the make or the plates. You?"

Dan shook his head. "Dark colored SUV, that's it."

Two paramedics crouched down, nudging Dan aside. One still wore a paper napkin tucked into the waist of his pants. He worked with calm efficiency.

"Hey Chief," the paramedic said, shining a light in Bains' eyes. "You interrupted my dinner break. There's a piece of Ruby's peach pie back on the table, calling my name." He smiled at Bains, checking for other injuries.

The second EMT took the chief's blood pressure on his left arm.

"Good thing we were right across the street." He put the pressure cuff back in the case and recorded something on a clipboard.

Bains swung his eyes up to the paramedic. "Did you see the car, Tom?"

"Afraid not. Sorry. I heard the bang, but by the time I got to the window you were lying in the street with this fellow here," he hooked his thumb in Dan's direction, "kneeling over you. We're going to need to transport you to Regional, Chief. Policy," he added before Bains could argue.

"You took a hit to the head. They'll want to check it out," napkin guy said, reaching over to pull the gurney closer before looking at Dan. "You and your friend should get looked at too."

"That's not necessary." Rebecca moved to stand next to Dan and held out her arm. "I can handle a scraped knee and elbow. Just take care of Chief Bains."

Bains called out instructions to his men even after the ambulance doors closed.

Dan went over and spoke to Officer Turner for a few minutes before coming back and taking her hand in his. "Come on," he said. "We're going to the hospital."

Rebecca rolled her eyes. "I'm fine Dan." She poked at the scrape on his shoulder through the tear of his shirt. "Ouch. That looks nasty."

"I'll feel better having you checked out." He leaned in to brush his lips across hers. "Besides, I want to try to get in to see Bains."

By the time they reached the hospital, Bains had been examined by doctors and given a temporary home behind a curtain while waiting to go to x-ray. Dan spoke briefly to the triage nurse, who situated Rebecca behind a curtain of her own with instructions to wait there.

"This really isn't necessary," she said, her nose crinkling. Dan grimaced at the overwhelming smell of antiseptic.

"Do it for me. Please." Dan raised her hand and kissed the scraped palm, melting any further resistance.

The nurse laughed. "It's not that busy tonight. A short wait to make a fellow like this happy is a small price to pay."

Another nurse poked her head between the curtains. "We could use you at the desk when you get a sec, Mary." She gave a quick smile to Rebecca, before leaving.

"Spoke too soon," Dan quipped.

The nurse laughed. "Looks like it."

He patted Rebecca's arm. "It shouldn't be long now. As soon as we're done here I want to try and get in to see Bains—"

Voices from the other side of the curtain cut Dan off.

"Are you sure you want to be making that kind of decision now, sir?"

"You questioning me, Turner?"

"No sir. But you did take a hit to the head."

Dan smiled and shook his head at Rebecca when a deep sigh traveled through the curtain panel. Some people never knew when to keep their mouths shut.

"It's my arm that's broke, not my head. Get back to the station, and get started on that before I give you another reason to be here."

"Yes, sir." The man mumbled something unintelligible as he passed outside Dan and Rebecca's curtain.

"That you, Chief?" Dan peeked through the gap in the curtains, and then drew them aside.

"How you holding up, Chief?" Rebecca asked as she hopped off the gurney and walked over to him.

"Doc says it's just a broken arm, and a slight concussion." He shrugged his shoulders. "I've had worse. I'll be back to work tomorrow. His eyes pierced Dan. "I thought I asked the two of you to stay out of trouble. Things keep getting more and more intriguing. First, a dead body, then someone uses you for target practice. Now a hit and run."

"What makes you think they were after us?" Dan stalled. "You were the one in the street."

"That car was aiming right for both of you. It almost jumped the damn curb when it swerved toward you at the last second. You know of anyone that wants to hurt you, son?" Rebecca's face whitened when Bains looked over to her. "You've got some pretty determined people sending you a message. I need to know what this is all about. Now."

Chief Bains hit the button to raise his bed. "You've brought me into this." He gestured to the sling on his left arm. "On a personal level. When I get out of here, I intend to kick some ass. If you don't want it to be yours, start talking."

Dan pulled a chair over and pressed on Rebecca's shoulder until she sat. He took a quick look out the curtain, and then hitched his hip on the end of the bed. "As we told you and Tate last week, Rebecca believes the body we found at Red Eye is somehow connected to her daughter's disappearance." Dan rested his hand on the back of Rebecca's neck. "We also shared with you how we came to know where the body could be found."

He sighed. "You did. And I hoped Rebecca would present a different option once she had a chance to think things over. Get to the parts I don't already know." Bains rested his head back and closed his eyes.

"We have a name that might belong to the body."

That brought the chief's head back up. His eyes narrowed as he looked toward Rebecca. "I suppose you're going to tell me this information came to you the same way the location of the body did?"

"It is what it is, Chief." Dan gave Rebecca's trembling hand a quick squeeze of support. "You either believe us or you don't."

"Give me the name."

"Nicole Wilson."

"That's not the answer I wanted to hear," he said, rubbing his eyes.

Dan closed his eyes.

Rebecca broke the silence. "That makes three children involved in this now. God."

"We don't know for sure they're connected," Dan corrected her. "We'll get to the answers a whole lot faster if we work together, chief. We have no motive other than to find Sabrina. It makes sense that the people behind her disappearance are trying to prevent that."

"You believe that's what this is all about?" Bains grimaced and shifted on the bed. "You're some kind of fancy PI now. You sure it's not a past case of yours? Some ex-con out for revenge? Or an irate husband who got caught cheating, maybe?"

"I know it isn't."

Bains rubbed his good hand over his face. "Shit. I don't really think you two are behind this mess, but I don't have another suspect at the moment." He closed his eyes for a bit and then sighed. "I want this bastard caught. What do you need from me?"

"A name to go with the body would help."

"We'll be releasing it to the press in a couple of days anyway, once the family's been notified. I don't see any harm in giving it to you now. The body is a seven year-old girl from a local family. They moved away before she went missing, so I didn't catch the case, didn't even know about it. The family lives in Phoenix now. Jennifer Reynolds. Happy little kid. Always smiling."

Rebecca gasped. "Oh my God, I remember them. John and Susan adopted her when Pete and I got married." The hand on her neck tightened, giving her strength. "They left town shortly after Bree went missing."

"Do you have a TOD?"

"Based on tests done so far, she's been in the ground about eighteen months."

"What about an address to go with that name?" Dan pushed.

Rebecca fished an old receipt and a pen from her purse and scribbled down the address Chief Bains gave them.

"Course, I'll be giving this same information to Phoenix P.D." Bains laid his head back again. "But not until I get more pain meds."

# Chapter Nine

Dan pulled the Cherokee to the curb in front of the small, single story house.

"No cars in the driveway." Rebecca reached for the door handle.

"That doesn't mean anything," Dan replied, coming around to meet with Rebecca. He stopped midway up the front walk and bent to fiddle with his sneaker.

"Um, Dan, your shoe's already tied."

His eyes lingered on her before moving past her to the next house. He smiled at her. "Right. Let's go then."

When no one answered their knock, Dan leaned over to peek through a split between the curtains. "Maybe they're out back, let's walk around, and check.

Rebecca hurried around the corner after him, and then stopped short. "Get back here," she hissed at his backside, as he hoisted himself up and disappeared through a side window. A moment later, his head and arms popped through from the other side. "I hope you're not about to suggest I break into that house with you."

"Of course not," he replied." You're going to come in through an open door at the back. Just go around there," he pointed, "and I'll be waiting for you."

"Dan, I told you I am not..." Rebecca whispered through the now open window. She rose up on her toes to peek in and saw Dan's backside again, this time turning the corner out of the bathroom and into the hallway. "Damn."

Dan waited around the corner. "What took you so long?"

She smacked his arm. "For a former FBI agent, sworn to uphold the law, you play pretty fast and loose with the rules," she whispered again.

He yanked her to him and planted a kiss on her lips. He grinned, led her into the house, and closed the back door behind them. "You're worth it." His expression turned serious as he scoped-out the small kitchen. "This doesn't look good."

Rebecca looked around. Crumbs scattered over the counter top, a few dirty dishes sat in the sink, and a couple of cupboard doors and drawers hung slightly open. She walked over to take a closer look. "This drawer's almost empty." She reached down and opened another one. "This one too."

He turned and headed down the hall, opening doors as he went. "Shit." Dan smacked his hand on the doorframe at the end of the hall. "They've skipped."

"How did they know we were coming?" Rebecca stopped beside him.

"Good question." Dan opened the closet while Rebecca checked the dresser drawers.

"They're gone, and they left in a hurry, taking what they could on short notice," Rebecca noted, dangling a tank top from her fingers.

"It makes me wonder how much notice they had."

"Meaning, did it originate from Cutter's Gulch, or from Phoenix?" Rebecca clarified.

"Exactly."

"My God, Dan," Rebecca sat on the bench at the foot of the bed, shoulders slumped. "How many people are involved in this?"

Dan crouched down and took her hands. "We're getting closer Rebecca, don't lose hope. Each day brings another clue." He stood, tugging her up with him. "Let's see if we can find one here."

They headed back toward the kitchen, looking in rooms as they went, pausing at the second bedroom. Decorated for a young child, the room had a teddy bear border, mauve paint, and white eyelet curtains on the window. Rebecca met Dan's surprised eyes. "They must have had another child. Another girl by the looks of it." Rebecca stood by the open closet door where she found a toy bin overflowing with pink and purple Lego Mega Blocks, and a few articles of clothing. Checking the price tag still hanging from the sleeve of a dress, she looked at Dan. "Size three! It's brand new, probably a gift she's already outgrown. Nothing else of note, no pictures, no mementos. Someone took extra time to pack up this room."

"Let's check out the living room, quickly, before we head out. We should be hearing from the neighbor soon."

Rebecca tilted her head. "Ah, when you checked your shoe, you were actually checking out the neighbor, weren't you?"

He dropped another quick kiss on her lips. "You're so clever." He walked to the living room window and peeked out. "Here she comes now, let's go." They sat in the shade of the patio umbrella when she waddled around the corner.

"Oh," she brought her hand to her chest, clearly taken aback to see them lounging in the back yard. She clasped the front edges of her terry cloth robe together, as close as they would fit over her swollen belly. "Hello, I'm Grace and you are—?"

"Looking for John and Susan Reynolds." Dan walked toward her, winning smile in place and hand outstretched in greeting.

The frown lines in her forehead burrowed deeper, and she struggled to hold the flaps closed while she shook his hand. "I'm Dan, and this is my wife, Becca. Nice to meet you."

"Um, yeah, sure. You too." She gave her head a slight shake. "They're not here."

"Oh darn. We were in the area and thought we'd drop in for a visit. Maybe they'll be back soon. We have time to wait a bit."

"You'll be waiting a while I'm afraid."

"Oh?" Dan held a chair out for her. "They didn't mention they were going away."

A grateful sigh escaped Grace as she eased her bulk into the chair. "Not to me either. They packed up most of their stuff in the middle of the night and left." She rubbed her hand over her stomach and smiled. "This little guy is nocturnal. I got up to see if a hot bath would settle him and maybe ease my swollen ankles. That's when I noticed the commotion over here."

"Maybe they had an early flight for their vacation."

She put her feet up on the chair Dan moved over. "Bless you," she whispered then shook her head. "They had that van fully loaded. Wherever they're going, they're driving. There's no way they're getting on an airplane with all that stuff, especially all of Tricia's toys."

"What a shame we missed them. I worked with John over in Cutter's Gulch before they moved here and all he talked about was his baby girl." Dan moved to stand behind Rebecca and rested his hands on her shoulders.

61

"I get the impression that John regrets moving from there."

"What makes you say that?"

She grinned. "He's always going on about the hiking and climbing he did there. Especially on a trail called Red Eye. I think he might have put on a few pounds since he left."

"I'll have to make sure that doesn't happen to me." Dan patted his stomach.

Rebecca rolled her eyes when Grace's gaze lingered on his very flat abs. The man was shameless.

"Now that we've moved here we looked forward to finally seeing Tricia. We've only seen her newborn pictures."

"Oh, well, I have a current picture of her I can show you." Grace managed to get herself up with a bit of help from Dan, and they headed around to the front of Grace's house.

While Grace went inside Rebecca turned to Dan. "Your wife?"

He grinned. "It seemed appropriate."

"What if she notices I'm not wearing a ring?"

"It took me a few minutes to find it. It's a family picture I took during Tricia's Easter egg hunt this year." Rebecca shoved her hands in her pockets, while Grace waddled over and handed the picture to Dan. "She's a real cutie, isn't she?"

Rebecca studied the picture Dan held in front of her, careful to keep her hands hidden. Brown hair tied in piglets, the smiling child hefted her overflowing Easter basket while mom and dad crouched in behind her. A picture perfect happy family.

"It's nice that she has the same coloring as John and Susan. It's hard to believe she's adopted."

Rebecca fought to hide her surprise at the news. "She's beautiful."

Dan held the picture out to Grace. "Thanks for showing us this and taking the time to chat with us. We'll have to catch up with them another time.

"You can keep it. I have dozens of pictures of Tricia." Grace shook Dan's hand again, and then reached out for Rebecca's. Rebecca pulled her right hand from her pocket and smiled at Grace. "Nice to meet you, and I hope Junior lets you get some sleep tonight."

With a laugh and a wave, Grace waddled back into her house.

Dan tucked the photo into the back pocket of his jeans and headed for the car. "Let's head home and see where we go from here."

"She seemed helpful."

His eyes went to the rearview mirror. "Maybe too helpful," he said and pulled away.

# Chapter Ten

One folded his hands against the front of his black robe, one over the other, and observed the nine figures surrounding the Blessing Stone from under the cover of his hood. The wind whistled through the tunnels of the old cave stirring their robes and teasing the ceremonial flames into a dance. Twelve knew his leader's way of silent observation from times past. They stood, heads bowed, awaiting the spit and sizzle of liquid hitting hot stone, the signal indicating the meeting would begin.

Twelve noticed One make a final inspection of the collective, pausing on the two empty spaces. Their leader shifted his hood toward the back of his head, revealing eyes flaring with a promise of retribution. Lifting the golden chalice from the table beside him, One smiled and let the blood spill.

"Our allegiance to thee," they chorused and raised their heads in unison. Nine and Seven broke away, lighting the fire sticks resting against the table, mounting them in crude holders attached to the cave walls.

"Do you have your report, Two?" One gestured to the figure on his right.

"There have been too many incidents, people are becoming suspicious. None of our attempts have worked, and continuing in the same manner might endanger our cause. We'll have to come up with another plan."

A murmur of ascent rumbled through the group.

"Rebecca is not easily discouraged." Seven's shaky voice revealed age and a touch of censure. He opened his mouth to continue and then closed it.

"What did you want to say Seven?" their leader prompted. "Come now, you are safe among us and well respected. We value your input. Share your thoughts."

"As you wish. There have been hints over the years," Seven's shaky voice continued, "suggesting she possesses ability previously unknown to us. She has a gift." Twelve watched One observe the group, as Seven continued. "I feel a resonance when she is nearby, much like the connection we have here."

"Our connection is forged through blood," Nine scoffed. "The implication is insulting and improbable." Several voices hummed in agreement.

"Of course, these are my own observations. Others may have differing opinions." Seven looked around the circle. "However, I know I'm not alone in my thoughts on this matter."

Twelve spoke up, but his voice cracked, sounding small and cautious to his own ears. "I, too, have felt this connection, as you call it, though I hesitate to use that word." The lack of argument gave his voice strength. "Rebecca has an energy about her that compliments ours." He smiled. "Yes, "compliments" is the word I would use." He kept his gaze steady on One. "I suggest we look into the possibility that she may have been missed."

A gasp echoed throughout the chamber, as nine sets of wary eyes turned to their leader.

One took his time replying, "The chosen ones have always been clearly marked." He looked at Three. "You have never indicated the presence of such a mark on her." His gaze swung to his left, to Five. "Nor you." An edge of steel hardened his voice. "Need I remind you that our collective is suffering at the betrayal of Six and Eleven as it is?" A low murmur swept through the group. "Do either of you have something you wish to tell us?"

"Not me," Five answered.

Three waited until he had the full attention of the collective. "I believe I have more than proven my loyalty." Robes shifted around the circle. "You know all that I know." Several hoods bobbed in support. "If Rebecca bears the mark it is nowhere I could see it."

"I am not convinced she is chosen." One paused a moment before uttering his next words toward Seven, "If she can do what you suspect, she could be a threat to us." Questioning eyes looked toward One. "The Collective cannot be put at risk. All threats must be eliminated."

Twelve struggled to hide his shock. "What are you saying?"

One stared at him. "If I said she must die," Twelve's right arm clutched at his chest when One's displeasure burned through him, "would that be a problem for you, Twelve?"

"No," he gasped, "of course not."

One took a deep breath before addressing the group. "I would like to see this threat eliminated," he looked into the ceremonial fire, "but, Twelve raises a valid point. We need to know for sure if she is a missed chosen one."

One looked to Five now. "You would be the logical one to take care of this, but we don't have much time left. If you can't make this happen soon, we will have to bring her in." He licked his lips. "You all know how much a power like hers would strengthen the collective if she turns out to be chosen. In either case, at the very least, she must be neutralized. If she bears the mark, she will take part in the ceremony, thus passing her powers to us. If there is no mark, an accident will be arranged."

"To a vote then." Two pulled a small drawstring bag from the folds of his robe, and passed it to Three, who reached in and retrieved a black stone, before handing the bag to the member next to him. Around it went, until each member of the collective held a small black stone in their grasp.

"Rebecca McKenney has become a threat to the collective. I vote that she be neutralized." One's eyes glittered as he tossed his stone into the fire.

"I vote that she be neutralized," Two repeated, throwing his stone into the circle. The vote continued, each voting in favor. Perspiration trickled down Twelve's back as his turn neared. *How the hell did things get so out of control?* Scaring her off gave him the chance to rescue her, and maybe she'd be grateful enough to notice him. But killing her? He wanted no part of it. Neutralization gave her a chance at least. Hearing the silence, Twelve looked up to find each of his brothers watching. Waiting. He lobbed his stone into the fire, cringing at the crackle of sparks that shot up. "I vote she be neutralized."

"And so it shall be done." One lifted the chalice and poured the remaining blood onto the fire.

The brothers went about the mundane task of closing out the meeting. Once they extinguished the fire and the torches, they switched to flashlights and filed out.

Twelve hung back, staring into the still smoldering embers. God help him, he couldn't go against them. If he did, he would be up for neutralization as the next threat. "I'm sorry," he whispered and made his way to the exit.

# Chapter Eleven

Rebecca picked up her lunch tray and headed toward Carrie, who somehow managed to snag the prized table by the window overlooking the fountain outside the hospital cafeteria.

Carrie shifted her tray over to make room for Rebecca's. "I'm so glad we finally have a moment to catch up, I've been working a lot of extra shifts lately." She waited for Rebecca to get settled. "It's been a crazy week for you. You doing okay?"

Rebecca sighed and glanced out the window, wishing she could confide everything in Carrie. "Crazy doesn't begin to cover it."

"I heard about Chief Bains." Carrie reached out and gripped Rebecca's fingers. "Is there any truth to the rumor the car that hit him meant to hit you and Dan instead?"

Rebecca pulled her hand away and kept her eyes on her egg-salad sandwich. "That's what Chief Bains suggested too, but Dan and I weren't even in the road. It's most likely someone unhappy with a parking ticket or something like that."

Carrie drew her hand back. "You're probably right," she said, waving her forkful of salad in the air. "It's not like you have any enemies. Who would want to hurt you?"

"Exactly," Rebecca said, biting into her sandwich.

Carrie leaned in, grinning. "So fill me in on the hunk." She licked her fingers and made a sizzling sound. "Ooh la la, he is one hot specimen. Is he good in bed?"

Somehow, Rebecca got the bite down her throat.

"Oh, don't go acting all Virgin Mary on me. You're a woman with needs, needs that have been sadly neglected for far too long."

Rebecca let a smile play on her lips. "He is kind of hot, isn't he?"

"Without question. But I really want to know if he can heat up the sheets. Give me details."

Rebecca shook her head, grateful to have a best friend to remind her to loosen up and have fun now and again. "I am not giving you details."

Carrie scrunched up her face and pushed her salad around on her plate. "You're no fun. I'm in a dry spell right now. I was hoping to live vicariously through you."

Rebecca laughed aloud, drawing curious stares from other diners. "Let's just say he's everything you're imagining—and more."

Carrie groaned and fanned her face with her hand. "Oh my God, I'm dying here." She leaned in, her expression serious now. "I'm so happy for you honey. You deserve this." She studied Rebecca for a moment more. "I know when something's bothering you. We tell each other everything. What are you keeping from me?"

Guilt tore through Rebecca. She told Dan this would never work, Carrie knew her too well. She scrambled for enough of the truth to satisfy Carrie, without breaking her promise to Dan. "You know about the body the chief identified?" She blinked rapidly when Carrie nodded. "Dammit, I can't believe I'm letting this get to me."

Carrie regarded her with solemn eyes. "It must have stirred up a lot of pain. If you want to lie down on the floor and have a tantrum right now it would be fine with me."

Rebecca rolled her eyes, giving a shaky laugh.

"Seriously." Carrie continued, "Anyone would understand. Did you wonder if it might be Sabrina?"

"Not for a minute." Guilt seeped in, because for a moment, when she'd realized what the shape in the bag could be, fear tore through her. "But you're right, it churned up a lot of bad stuff. I remember Jennifer Reynolds. I remember the day John and Susan brought her home. In fact, Susan recommended the agency they used when Pete and I decided to adopt."

"Convince me you won't let this send you into a downward spiral again." Carrie leaned in. "You've worked so hard to get this far. You're finally allowing yourself to trust a man again. Dan seems to be exactly what you need right now. Don't hate me for saying this," she hesitated, "but you need to let go of the past so you can move on."

Rebecca sighed and pulled back. "I'll never let go of Bree, you know that." This time Carrie looked out the window, evading her eyes. "But I don't hate you. I know you have my best interests at heart. We're good, okay."

Carrie nodded, her eyes focused somewhere beyond Rebecca's left shoulder. "We're good. Dr. Laramie is booking physicals today. It reminded me that you're due for one. It's been a couple of years, you should come in soon." Carrie frowned at Rebecca's stubborn silence and added, "Especially now that you're sexually active again."

Rebecca's jaw dropped.

"Are you even taking birth control? I bet he hasn't been celibate. Are you using protection?"

Rebecca gave in and laughed. She knew better than to try to stop one of Carrie's rants. "What? Are you my mother now?"

"Someone has to look out for you. Think about it, okay? Every woman needs a physical every couple of years, you know that. Don't be stupid about it."

"Thank you Nurse Carrie." Rebecca glanced at her watch. "When do you have to be back to work?"

With a squeak, Carrie jumped up. "Crap, this is the third time I've been late this week, Laramie's going to kill me. Think about what I said. Love ya, bye." She started to gather things on her tray.

"Leave it. Let's get together for some girl time soon, I've missed that."

"You're on. Call me," she called over her shoulder and headed toward the bank of elevators.

\* \* \* \*

Rebecca ran a few errands before meeting Dan at her place and leaving for the city. After digging out the paperwork from Bree's adoption, she gave the package to Dan. Brindle's Adoption Agency appeared legit up front, but Rebecca knew Dan asked Jones, one of his team at Anderson, to look deeper. They made the drive into the city in silence. Rebecca spent the time dealing with nerves and a roiling stomach.

They went over the game plan the night before, and he coached her through possible questions and appropriate responses. Rebecca smiled to herself as she shook her head. She couldn't believe Dan agreed to her idea of posing as an adoptive couple. He resisted at first, wanting to wait until he received the full report back from Ryker Jones. Something she said must have changed his mind since they had a four o-clock appointment with the agency director, Vanessa Ridgeway.

Dan parked, and then reached over to rub his thumb along her lips. "Nervous?"

"Maybe a little."

His hand cupped her cheek to hold her in place when she would have turned away. "Babe, if you don't want to do this, say the word and we're out of here."

Eyes closed, she let her cheek rest in the cradle of his hand, inhaling the faint scent of lavender. Rebecca loved floral soaps and it only occurred to her now that she had them by every sink in the house. She'd have to find something a little less girly. She smiled and pressed a kiss to his palm. "I'm ready, let's go in."

The offices looked the same, sporting shades of soft blue and taupe. Two love seats offered a place where anxious couples could draw comfort from one another while they waited to talk to someone with the power to change their lives. Rebecca remembered sitting there, clutching Pete's hand in hers.

Pulling herself back to the present, she approached the desk. The receptionist, young, stacked, and very blond, greeted them as soon as they entered. "Hello there, you must be Rebecca and Dan." Her warm smile put Rebecca at ease, which is probably part of the reason they hired her, Rebecca thought. "You're our last appointment of the day. Ms. Ridgeway will see you shortly."

Rebecca pulled a thick folder of papers out of her satchel and gave it to the receptionist. "We filled out the pages you emailed us. Is there anything else you need from us?"

"We still have your past paperwork on file." She looked briefly at Dan. "Ms. Ridgeway will make note of any changes during your meeting, and I'll update the paperwork for your next appointment."

Dan extended his hand. "I'm Dan Cooper. It's nice to meet you."

"Oh, well, thank you Mr. Cooper." She smiled, clearly flustered. "And I'm Stacey. Is there anything I can get you while you're waiting? Coffee? Water?" Stacey looked down at the flashing light on her phone. "It looks like Ms. Ridgeway is ready for you now." She picked up the file Rebecca had given her and started down the hall. "I'll take you back."

Dan rested his hand at the small of Rebecca's back as they followed. Stacey stopped at the entry to the office and gestured for them to precede her. "Are you sure I can't get you anything?" she asked Dan as he passed.

"Nothing, thanks, we're fine."

"That will be all Stacey," Vanessa Ridgeway added.

Stacey placed the file on the desk, then left, closing the door behind her.

Taking a deep breath, Rebecca turned to greet Vanessa Ridgeway. Her elegant blond topknot and cream silk suit spelled class, and the patent LaButon's screamed money. But deep lines bracketed her eyes and settled around her mouth. Rebecca recognized the signs of stress and hard living.

"How nice to see you again." Vanessa stepped forward to take both of Rebecca's hands in hers, briefly rubbing over the bare finger on the left hand before turning to Dan. "And you must be Rebecca's fiancé."

"Dan Cooper, yes, nice to meet you Ms. Ridgeway."

She returned to her desk and lowered herself into her leather chair. "Please, have a seat." She waved her hand at the two sky blue padded armchairs and picked up the file Stacey placed on the desk. "I understand you're interested in adopting again." She flipped though the folder as she spoke, turning a page before lifting her gaze to Rebecca. "I'm sure you remember the intensive screening we did last time." At Rebecca's nod, she continued, "We'll have to repeat the process, as several things in your life have changed since then." She looked pointedly at Dan.

"Of course, I would expect nothing less," Dan responded.

She returned her gaze to Rebecca. "We'll perform the psychological exams again as well." She blinked her dry eyes several times. "Losing a child is traumatic. I'm very sorry for your loss."

"Thank you," Rebecca choked out.

"Forgive my bluntness, but it's my job to put the children first. Our doctors will need to be sure you're ready to adopt again and not simply replacing," she checked the folder, "Sabrina, with another child."

"I can assure you." Rebecca's knuckles whitened on the armrests of the chair. "There's nothing simple about this. I am in no way attempting to replace my daughter. As you can see, I'm entering a new phase of my life," she looked at Dan, "and starting over. We're both eager to start a family together."

"Of course dear." The smile never reached her eyes. "Procedure and all that. You understand. I'll review your file and get back to you. I'm afraid we don't have any infants at the moment. You may have a long wait ahead of you." She closed the folder and leaned back in her chair.

Dan stood. "Thank you for your time, we'll see ourselves out."

Rebecca followed Dan through the empty reception area and out to the car.

"That woman had a hate-on for you before you even walked in. Nothing you said would have made a difference."

"Pete and I liked her when we came in to adopt Bree." Rebecca shot him a look from the corner of her eye. "She's changed. Maybe it's you she doesn't like."

"Very funny. She's hiding something that's for sure. Look." Dan nodded at the receptionist who stood next to her car fishing in her oversized hobo bag for her keys. "Looks like it's quitting time. I'm betting she'll be more open to conversation than your Ms. Ridgeway."

"She will if you're the one doing the asking," Rebecca teased. "She sure took a shine to you." A flush spread up his face. "Oh my God, are you embarrassed Mr. Macho FBI Man?" She laughed.

Putting the car in gear, he pulled out behind Stacey. "Just drop it," he muttered, making her laugh even harder.

A few minutes later Dan turned left onto Third and followed Stacey into the Coach & Willie's parking lot. "We're in luck. Looks like she needs a drink after a long day at work."

"Maybe we can make that work to our advantage," Rebecca said, meeting him in front of the car. "Seems reasonable that we would want to grab a quick bite close by before the long drive home." Rebecca looped her arm through Dan's. "Shall we?"

Dan's eyes heated. "You are so my kind of woman," he growled, pulling her to him for a quick, intense kiss. She groaned when he pulled away. "I intend to take this up where we left off when we get home."

Home. It sounded so good when he said it. "I'll hold you to that."

Coach & Willie's enjoyed an after work rush. It seemed like most of Phoenix felt the need to take the edge off their busy week this fine Friday evening.

Rebecca spotted the receptionist at the bar and headed for a booth close by. Stacey checked her watch and looked toward the door. Whoever she planned to meet better hurry up, Rebecca thought. Stacey didn't seem the type to wait long.

Dan got up and walked to stand next to her at the bar, while Rebecca watched. Flagging the bartender down, he ordered a draft and a sweetened iced tea and looked around while he waited.

"Oh, hi there, remember me?"

Dan looked down. "Stacey isn't it?" He smiled. "Hi there yourself. Small world."

"I hope your appointment at Brindle's went well."

"It could have gone better, if you really want to know. I don't think the dragon lady liked us very much." He slapped his hand over his mouth. "I am so sorry. I never should have said that." Rebecca grimaced, a little perturbed at how well he lied.

Stacey laughed and leaned in close, causing the loose folds of her blouse to gape open. "Don't worry about it." When the bartender set her glass of red down, Stacy paused to take a sip. "Truth be told, I often think of her the same way."

"Looks like you really needed a drink tonight."

She looked up from beneath lowered lashes. "You don't know the half of it." She checked her watch again and frowned.

"Are you waiting for someone?"

"Not for much longer." Wine sloshed over the rim when her glass hit the bar.

Dan picked up the drinks he ordered and turned to the booth. Rebecca waved back at them. He laid his winning smile on Stacey. "You're welcome to you join us while you wait."

"Really?" She picked up her glass of wine. "If you're sure."

"Hello again." Rebecca took the glass Dan handed her. "Seems like we all had the same idea tonight." She slid over to make room for Stacey, who slid in beside Dan instead. Rebecca rolled her eyes and then winced when Dan's foot connected with her ankle under the table.

"Anyway." Dan turned to Stacey. "We're not sure if Brindle's is the agency for us. Ms. Ridgeway said you have no infants available."

Stacey frowned. "That's odd. We had two expectant moms referred to us this week alone."

"Is that how you get most of the children?" Rebecca prompted. "Through expectant moms?"

"Some yes. There are always orphans, of course, but they tend to be older. The infants are usually young mothers, teens mostly, who decide to give up their children for their own good," she said. *Probably misquoting the New Employee handbook,* Rebecca thought.

"We figured we might stand a better chance if we considered an older child," Dan fished. "Maybe three to five years old?"

"Oh, well, you'd definitely do better with that. We get a lot that age. Mostly girls though." She looked at Dan, her eyes sending mixed messages. "Are you looking for a girl?"

Rebecca cleared her throat, and Stacey flushed. "A girl would be wonderful," Rebecca answered for Dan. "Do you know if you have any available at this time?"

"Well, one missed her appointment this week." She shrugged. "But we'll have another one soon, we always do." She looked toward the door and called out to the twenty-something blond man checking his reflection in the window. "There's my friend," she said, sliding away from Dan regretfully. She rummaged in her bag for her wallet.

"It's on us," Dan said. "I hope your weekend gets better from here on out.

She laughed, already moving on to the next best thing. "Oh it will. Thanks."

"She certainly got over you in hurry." Rebecca batted her lashes at him. "Guess you're just too old for her." The look on his face promised retribution. She couldn't wait.

"There's a distinct pattern emerging here, are you seeing it?"

"Girls, three to five years old?" Rebecca sent a bitter smile his way. "Yeah, I see it. The abducted children we're looking for have families though."

"That we know of."

"True enough," Rebecca continued. "But wouldn't it make more sense to target the kids who don't get adopted? It would be a hell of a lot easier, especially if the agency is involved."

"And a lot more suspect," Dan countered. "The Bureau would be all over them. Besides, I'm not convinced that Brindle's is involved yet. They're up to something for sure," Dan said as Rebecca scoffed in disbelief, "but only Bree and Jennifer were adopted. Nicole Wilson lived with her birth parents."

Rebecca shook her head. "Nicole had to be involved in this. Seeing her picture is what triggered my visions."

"Maybe she's served her purpose. There doesn't have to be any other connection."

Rebecca rubbed her temples. "Let's run through this again. I saw Nicole's picture, had a vision of her looking slightly different, went home, and had a vision of Bree. The next vision showed four people burying a body on the mountain. That body turns out to be Jennifer Reynolds."

Dan held a hand up. "Whoa, back up a bit. You said Nicole looked slightly different in the vision than she did in the picture." He pulled the notebook out of his pocket and flipped through it quickly. "You didn't mention that before."

She rubbed her forehead now, trying to remember. "She looked older, like with the vision of Bree, and a mess. Her hands and face dirty, her clothes torn and bloody. That's all I meant."

"Are you sure you have the right child?"

Rebecca stared at him. "Of course I am. Maybe. Dammit Dan, you have me second guessing myself here." Rebecca closed her eyes and concentrated. "All three of them have similar coloring and hair. Bree I'm sure of, of course, and the police identified Jennifer." Rebecca nodded her head. "It's Nicole in the vision."

"I think it's time to bring in the team." Dan pulled out his wallet. "This is getting too big for us to handle on our own."

# Chapter Twelve

Dan called various team members from his office, while Rebecca laid things out in the meeting room. He reviewed his notes one last time before heading down the hall.

"I've managed to reach everyone except Kaden, who's out on assignment." Dan leaned against the doorframe. "They should start trickling in any time now."

"I don't think I've heard you mention him."

"Her. Kaden Tucker. She's quiet, small, and good at sneaking up on people. I swear, sometimes she's invisible."

"I'm surprised so many are available on a Friday night." Dan admired the view as Rebecca bent over to get dishes out of the credenza.

"A call doesn't go out very often, but when it does, the team's there." He avoided the swat of Rebecca's hand as he swiped a chicken wing from the Coach & Willie's container on the table. "Great idea to order food before we left," he mumbled around the wing. "These guys like to eat."

"Feed me, and I'll be yours forever." Rebecca's gaze was drawn by a male voice to the doorway where the newcomer smiled at the array of food. Even from her spot several steps away, she had to crane her neck back to see his face.

Dan smiled at the way Rebecca's eyes widened at the sight of Finn. He had a similar reaction the first time they met. Damn, the man is big. Finn walked over to cuff Dan on the shoulder before turning to face Rebecca.

"Are you going to introduce me to the lovely lady, Cooper?"

"Rebecca McKenney, meet Sean Finnegan."

Finn's hand swallowed Rebecca's. "All the pretty ladies call me Finn."

Dan frowned at the sudden thickening of Finn's Irish brogue. *Take a born flirt, add the striking combination of black hair and blue eyes, and you've got a damn chic magnet.*

Rebecca laughed and handed Finn a plate. "If it's hungry you are, dig in."

Finn laid his left hand on Rebecca's shoulder and took the plate with his right. "Why don't you tell me what we have in this fine spread?"

"You've been feeding yourself for a while now." Dan thumped Finn on the back and received an innocent look in return. "You can pick out your own food."

"What's this about food?"

"Hold on there, Ryker," Finn said. "Give the rest of us a chance to get some before you polish it off." He winked at Rebecca. "That man is always eating. Don't know where he puts it all, he's a skinny little bugger."

Dan laughed. Ryker may be lean, but he was all muscle.

Ryker ignored Finn and walked over to where Rebecca stood, Dan close beside her.

"Ryker Jones," he shook her hand.

"We spoke on the phone," Rebecca said. "It's nice to put a face to the name."

"That it is." His eyes met Dan's over Rebecca's shoulder. "I have that report for you."

Dan nodded. "We'll go over it when Evan and Nick get here." He glanced over Ryker's shoulder. "There he is now." Dan waved him over. "Rebecca, Nick Jameison."

"I understand now why Dan wanted to work alone with you on this case."

"Yeah," Finn called from the other side of the table. "Because he didn't want any witnesses when he crashed and burned." Laughter erupted in the room.

Ryker grabbed a plate and muscled his way in front of Finn. "Hey." Finn smacked the back of his head. "I got here first." Ryker just plucked an onion ring from Finn's plate and bit into it. Finn moved to shoulder-butt Ryker when Evan walked in.

"Now boys, play nice. We've got company." He walked over and shook Rebecca's hand. "Evan Anderson and I'm afraid this unruly bunch is mine." Turning, he addressed the group. "Grab your food and find a place to sit." He raised his voice to be heard over the chaos. "Let's get this meeting started."

The men continued to grumble and taunt one another while filling their plates, but quickly settled into working mode once they took their seats.

Evan gestured to Dan. "Bring us up to date."

Dan handed out the folders he collected from his office earlier. "I've given a general report to everyone and more detailed information to each of you in your particular field of expertise." Dan gave a brief explanation of the events over the last month while the team took a quick look through the folders. He picked up the report Ryker brought. "Ryker, what did you find out about Brindle's?"

"They've been in business for twenty years this September with an average turnover in staff, mostly admin support people. Donald Pratt served as director for the first five years, until he died of a heart attack, and Vanessa Ridgeway took on the role.

"They file their tax returns on time and have a good relationship with the various government agencies they report to. Child Protection Services claims Brindle's is one of the better agencies they work with. The money flow is what you'd expect, nothing extra coming in or going out. On the surface, they run a clean operation."

"And below the surface?"

Ryker leaned back in his seat. "Ridgeway has expensive taste. She makes good money as Director given her years there, but not much above industry standard. A woman of modest means, she's never been married. No inheritance found so far. I have several feelers out. I did a quick check of other agencies in this area of the country. While several demonstrate questionable ethics, none appear to have any connection to Brindle's or to this case."

Dan looked to Finn. "Anything on the ballistics from the Red Eye scene?"

"No matches. The guy used a standard twelve-gauge, nothing unusual about it, except, of course that he missed." He snickered. "An idiot would find it hard to miss at that distance, which supports your warning theory. Find me the gun, and I'll get you a match through ballistics. Until then I've got nothing."

Dan's gaze spanned around the table. He served with most of these guys. They're the best at what they do, with an uncanny knack for digging up hard to come by information.

"Questions? Thoughts?" he asked the group.

Nick wiped his hands on his napkin before picking up his folder. "A number of players are involved here. They're organized and well spread out." He tossed the napkin on his plate. "What's the motivation?" His eyes met Dan's first, then softened as they moved to Rebecca. "We're about to hit on sensitive subject matter for you ma'am. You might want to step out."

Seated next to Rebecca, Dan reached over and covered the hand in her lap with his own beneath the table. He felt warmth slowly return to her icy fingers, and heard her breathing slow as she relaxed.

"I've been living this nightmare for three years gentlemen. I promise you, I've envisioned every imaginable scenario at one point or another. I try not to dwell on them, with varying degrees of success." She met each of their gazes directly, making no effort to hide her fear. "We're talking suppositions here, I can handle it. It would be easy for me to leave the room now. I'll stay, if it's all the same to you." Dan opened his mouth to argue then thought better of it. "If I feel the need," Rebecca conceded, "I'll leave. Until then I'm staying."

Respect flickered over Nick's face and several others' around the table.

At Dan's nod, Nick continued, "If Nicole, Jennifer, and Sabrina are all connected, what's the payoff? It isn't money. No one ever offered ransom demands. The kids are held, or at least discarded, too close to home for trafficking. To be on the safe side, though, we should toss a few nibbles into that cesspool and see what floats to the surface."

Evan scratched something on the page in front of him. "I know a guy. I'll get a message to him and see if there's anything to that angle." Dan would bet his next paycheck there would be an answer on his desk by morning. Evan knew a lot of guys.

"I'd like to play with the time line, pick apart the pattern. We're missing a chunk of the puzzle."

"You've detected a pattern then?" Evan looked up from his notes.

Nick nodded. "Jennifer Reynolds disappeared eighteen months after Nicole Wilson. We're looking at almost the same period of time before Sabrina went missing."

"If the pattern continues as you're suggesting," Ryker interrupted, "we'll find evidence of another victim eighteen months after Sabrina." He pulled his laptop out of the bag hanging on the back of the chair and went to work. "I'm on it."

"How can this many children go missing from the same general area of the country and the Bureau not pick up on it?" Rebecca asked.

Ryker looked up from his laptop. "The FBI has an extensive and sophisticated network of support databases, as do the Police. They're great tools, but they're not infallible." He linked his fingers together and stretched his arms out in front of him, grinning. "What they don't have, is me."

While Ryker worked, Nick sketched a rough graph. "We know Jennifer died roughly three years post disappearance. Without another DB we can only guess at how the rest of the pattern will play out."

"DB?" Rebecca asked.

"Damn." Nick hung his head. "That would be dead body."

"I see." She managed a tight smile. "And you think there's another DB out there now, specifically Nicole Wilson?" Silence. "And you believe when her body is found, it will show she died three years after her abduction. Would this fit with your pattern?" A collection of expletives whispered throughout the room.

Rebecca shrugged off the hand Dan placed on the back of her neck. "I keep saying Bree's been gone three years now, but that's not entirely accurate. It's been two years, eleven months and two days." Rebecca paused to swallow. "Which means Sabrina will die sometime in the next twenty eight days."

"Shit," Finn's voice lost all evidence of a brogue. "This isn't a confirmed pattern, Rebecca. Don't be jumping to conclusions we haven't reached yet."

Rebecca ignored him. "Why the overlap?"

"What overlap?" Evan asked Nick.

"She's right. If," Nick looked at Rebecca, "and that's a big if at this point, these kids were taken by the same perp," Nick glanced down at his makeshift chart, "there's an eighteen month overlap where they have two girls at the same time. When one," he paused and cleared his throat, "goes away, another replaces her."

Dan stood and started pacing. "Nick, find me a reason for keeping two girls at once."

Nick shot a quick glance at Rebecca. "Sure thing."

"Anything on that search yet, Ryker?"

Ryker's fingers flew over the keys. "Fifteen possibles, but none that fit all the criteria. I'll broaden the search area."

"One other thing." Nick waited until all eyes shifted to him. "If this is the pattern, they'll need to acquire another child by the end of the month." He didn't bother adding what every person in the room knew. They had twenty eight days to find these bastards, or Rebecca would lose her daughter forever.

* * * *

Rebecca pulled up in front of Ruby's and checked her reflection in the visor mirror. Remnants of yesterday's eyeliner framed bloodshot eyes, highlighting the fatigue within. Licking her finger, she did her best to minimize the smudges around her lashes, but nothing would erase the shadows beneath. She leaned in to make sure she hadn't missed a spot and caught sight of the car parked behind her.

"Shit." She rested her head on the steering wheel. "The last thing I need after a night of no sleep is to run into Pete. Especially looking like this." Rebecca needed full armor to face Pete's callous insensitivity on a day like today. Nothing created a shield like makeup. Her tendency to not carry any in her purse came back to bite her in the butt now. Digging deeper, she found a tube of the tinted lip balm she used to help with the damage from biting her lips. She applied a whisper-thin coat of color and pressed her lips together to blend.

"It'll have to do." She tossed the balm into the top of her bag. Taking a breath of courage, she opened the door.

She glanced through the passenger window as she passed Pete's car, her jaw dropping at the mess. Take-out wrappers and crushed soda cans littered the passenger seat. Rebecca placed her hand on the glass to get a better look when she saw the open package of cigarettes between the seats. "Since when did you start smoking Pete?" Rebecca shook her head and walked on. "Not my problem anymore," she muttered, opening the diner door.

The first smile of the day broke across her face when she took a deep breath on her way to the counter. The sweet smell of cinnamon and sugar slid straight to her stomach. The taste of Ruby's cinnamon buns had tickled her taste buds since she started pacing the floor at two in the morning, and the feeling only intensified as the night dragged on.

Ruby frowned, glancing to the back of the diner, before making her way over. "This is a surprise." She managed a genuine, if somewhat unsteady, smile.

"You can relax Ruby. I know Pete's slithering around here somewhere." Rebecca patted Ruby's hand as she sat on the barstool. "I'm not here to make a scene. I just came by for a box of cinnamon buns to take home with me."

The look of dismay on Ruby's face would have been comical, if Rebecca were in a mood to laugh.

"I'm sorry honey, I just served the last one."

Rebecca's eyes narrowed as she turned her head toward the table in the back and watched Pete lick the sticky remains off his fingers. He smiled as he wiped his hands before throwing some bills on the table. She turned narrowed eyes back to Ruby.

"I've got my Apple Jumble Muffins you like so much steaming on the counter. How 'bout I pack up a box of those for you instead?"

"That would be fine Ruby, thank you," she spat out. Judging by Ruby's speed, she wanted Rebecca out of there almost as bad as Rebecca wanted to be gone.

"Morning Becky."

She hated that nickname, a fact Pete knew. I'm an adult, she thought, taking another deep breath. I can be big about this.

"Pete." She nodded, then buried her head in her bag digging for her wallet.

"How've you been keeping?"

She slanted her eyes at him without stopping. "Fine."

"I hear you're shacking up with that Special Agent who drilled us when Sabrina went missing."

Rebecca ignored him. His loud sigh made her pause briefly, but she kept digging.

"I always found him a bit odd, but I feel the same way about you." His fingers drummed on the counter next to her purse.

Rebecca opened her wallet and placed some bills on the counter.

"What kind of cake are you making this year?" His lips curled up in a parody of a smile.

She spun to face him. He knew damn well she made a chocolate birthday cake every year, Bree's favorite, and threw every bloody one in the garbage, uneaten. "What do you care?"

His eyes widened, and his right hand went to his heart. "She was my daughter too, Rebecca."

"Is." Rebecca bit out. "Present tense."

"Sooner or later the facts are going to slap you in the face, and you'll be wondering what hit you," Pete leaned in and whispered, before raising his voice and looking around to make sure his captive audience didn't miss anything. "You need to get past this Rebecca."

"Don't tell me what I need to do."

"Someone has to. If Sabrina came home today, you wouldn't be a fit mother to her anyway. Christ Rebecca, you ordered happy face pancakes for her in the back booth just yesterday." He reached over and tapped her temple three times with his fingertip. "You're losing it babe, you need to go back to your shrink."

Rebecca's purse went flying when her arm swung up to shove his hand away. "Don't. Ever. Touch. Me. Again." She bent down and began shoving things into her purse. Tears clouded her eyes, and she kept her head bowed until she could blink them dry.

"Sorry for the disturbance, folks."

Rebecca glanced up to see Pete's arms spread wide, palms up in question.

"She clearly needs more time to get over losing our daughter."

Rebecca stood up and shoved him hard enough that he lost his balance, skidding back a step. "I did not lose her, you asshole," Rebecca's finger punctuated each word on his chest with sharp jabs, "and she's not your daughter, thank God." She ignored the gasps and the scraping of chairs as people jockeyed for better positions. "Your name may be on the adoption papers, but you don't deserve to be called a father." Rebecca swiped at the moisture under her nose. "A father would

84

never give up on his child. What you are, is a heartless bastard."

Fire shot from Pete's eyes, but he banked it when the crowd shuffled closer. "On second thought, I suggest you find a new shrink," he shook his head in feigned pity before running his eyes over the crowd. "Your last one obviously didn't help you at all."

Rebecca watched the door close behind him before blindly grabbing the box Ruby pressed in her hands.

"You never mind what he said dear. Just go on home and share these with that man of yours, and forget you ever saw Pete here."

Rebecca nodded, lifting her gaze just long enough to see the empty spot where Pete's car had been before rushing to the exit.

# Chapter Thirteen

Rebecca picked up the dip and nudged the oven door closed with her hip. "Can you grab the bowl?"

"Mmhm," Carrie mumbled around the warm tortilla chip she popped into her mouth. They duck-walked over and set the food on the coffee table next to their drinks, then sat down, stretching their legs out to admire freshly polished toes.

Carrie leaned forward and snagged a generous scoop of cheese dip. "I am so glad you changed your mind about tonight. When is the hunk expected back?"

"Not for a few hours yet, we've got plenty of girl time left." Rebecca leaned her head back on the sofa and sighed as she rubbed her temples. She opened her eyes to find Carrie watching her.

"Another one of your headaches?"

Rebecca winced. She'd have to do better at hiding her stress to fake her way through this night. "Nothing I can't handle." She picked up the stack of DVDs Carrie brought with her and flipped through them. When Harry Met Sally, The Notebook, The Devil Wears Prada. A laugh escaped at the last title. "Twilight?"

"You haven't seen it yet? Do you live under a rock? Robert Pattinson is hot!"

"He's also about twelve years old."

Carrie rolled her eyes. "Five bucks you won't be saying that after the movie."

"Twilight it is then."

"I have to get my romantic fix somewhere," Carrie grumbled, flopping back against the couch. "Why is it so hard to find a decent man?"

"Your crazy work hours might have something to do with that." Rebecca opened the case and stooped to put the disk in the DVD player.

The stab of pain hit the instant her fingers connected with the silver disk. Her bottom sank to the floor and panic overcame her as she gazed in Carrie's direction.

"What is wrong with you Rebecca?" Carrie knelt beside her.

"I'm sorry. I'll be okay soon." Her eyes closed as she lay on the floor.

"Rebecca? Come on Rebecca, wake up." Carrie lightly smacked her cheeks.

*Bree's voice came to her first. "Daddy? Daddy is that you?" Then sobbing. "Daddy, come back, I need you. Oh, daddy, not you too."*

*Pete? Why would Pete be there? Had he been taken too? The room slowly came into focus. Cold and barren, but for the cot, a threadbare blanket, and Bree. A bare bulb hung from the low ceiling, a string dangling down from it. The cot rested in the middle of the windowless room, directly beneath the light, instead of in the shadows against the wall. Bree was afraid of the dark.*

*Rebecca's heart broke at the sight of Bree sitting on the cot, hugging the blanket, and sucking her thumb, a habit she'd already outgrown.*

All too fast, the room flickered, and then faded away. "*No!*" Rebecca cried.

When she came to, Carrie's back was to her. She mumbled something before flipping the phone closed. Her face whitened when she turned and saw Rebecca's eyes open.

"You're awake, thank God." Carrie helped her sit up and rest her back against the side of the chair. She brushed the hair back from Rebecca's face.

"I'm sorry if I scared you."

"Terrified is more like it." Carrie sat on the floor across from her. "Can you tell me what happened?"

Her visions were the one secret she kept from Carrie, other than the real reason Dan moved in. Rebecca looked at the phone in Carrie's hand. "Did you call Dan?"

"What?" She looked down at her phone. "Oh, no, I never had a chance. I grabbed my phone in a panic then realized I didn't have Dan's number programmed so I ran to find yours. By the time I got back you woke up."

"It's only been a couple of minutes then?"

Carrie eyed her strangely. "Yes, four, maybe five minutes."

"I know you want an explanation. I'm not sure I can give it to you."

"That was no epileptic seizure or anything else I've encountered in my years as a nurse. And I've seen some pretty strange things." Her eyes narrowed. "What does Pete have to do with anything?"

Rebecca froze. "Pete?"

"Yeah, Pete. You called out his name a couple of times."

Rebecca sighed. "I could use a glass of water. Would you mind?"

Carrie's eyes flickered briefly to the glass of tea on the coffee table. "Of course not. Be right back."

Dan came in the front door as Carrie disappeared into the kitchen. "Oh no."

"Don't say anything about the visions," she whispered in his ear when he stooped down to lift her onto the couch.

"Thank goodness you're here," Carrie said, coming back into the room and handing Rebecca the glass of water.

"I managed to tie things up in Phoenix sooner than expected." Sitting down, he grabbed hold of Rebecca's hand and pressed his lips against the back of it. He looked at the munchies and the stack of movies. "I'm glad I finished up early."

"I don't understand what happened." Carrie sat in the adjacent chair. "One minute she's fine. The next thing I see, she's collapsing to the floor." Carrie looked at Dan. "She blacked out for several minutes." Carrie clasped a hand over her mouth and swung her gaze to Rebecca. "Oh my God, are you pregnant?"

Dan released Rebecca's hand to pass the box of tissues on the end table to Carrie. "Your nose is bleeding."

"Shit." Carrie dabbed at her nose and looked at the blood soaked tissue. "Must be allergies. I should be going anyway. Forget what I said. It's none of my business." Carrie grabbed her purse from the front hall table. "We'll do this another time." She spun around and headed out the door before Rebecca could say goodbye. They listened to the rumble of Carrie's Mustang as she revved the engine before driving away.

"Just another girl's night in the McKenney household?" He shifted Rebecca again, this time sideways onto his lap. "Why doesn't Carrie know about your visions?"

Rebecca leaned her head on Dan's chest. "It never came up."

"Seriously?" His chin bobbed up and down at her nod. "It never occurred to you that a best friend might offer comfort and support?"

"Or maybe just walk away in disgust. And fear," Rebecca mumbled into his chest.

Dan rubbed his hand in circles over her back. His lips brushed against her hair. "I hate that you went through this alone."

"My burden, my choice," she said around a yawn.

"Tell me about the vision, and then we'll get you to bed." He tilted her face up to his and kissed away the lone tear.

Rebecca explained the images. "Sabrina wasn't calling for him to come save her. It's more like he'd been there." She rubbed her temples again. "A lot of interference appeared with this one, like getting bad reception on the television."

Dan pulled his cellphone out of his pocket and hit a key. "Ryker, I need you to find Pete Hayes." Dan listened a moment. "All of his movements going back a couple of months if possible." He laughed. "Someday someone's gonna trample on that ego of yours. Tomorrow is good, thanks."

"Why would they take Pete?"

"Maybe he's been digging around too. Maybe he got too close to the truth and had to be stopped."

She shook her head. "I don't believe it. Pete's the one always telling me to admit that Bree's gone and move on. He believes she's dead. Why would he suddenly start looking for her?"

"The only way we'll know for sure is to ask him."

Rebecca yawned again. "I think it's time for bed." She covered her mouth with the back of her hand.

Dan's arms tightened around her. "Uh-uh," he said. "There's one more thing we need to discuss first." He moved one of his hands so it rested on her abdomen. "Is there any truth to what Carrie blurted out before she left? Could you be pregnant?"

Crap. She hoped he'd forget that part. Rebecca slid off Dan's lap and sat sideways to face him, her right leg hooked over her left ankle. "There's a reason Bree's adopted."

Dan rested his elbow on the back of the couch and ran his fingers through her hair. "People adopt for lots of reasons, Rebecca. What were yours?"

"We couldn't have children."

"Because of Pete, or because of you?"

"It's a team effort Dan."

His hand gripped the back of her neck and gave a gentle shake. "Don't be stubborn. Did Pete have a low sperm count, or were you unable to conceive? Were you both tested?"

Rebecca sighed. "Yes, and it appears the problem lies with me." She pulled her neck away from his hand. "Satisfied?"

His hand connected with the back of her neck again. "No. What did the doctor say? Specifically," he added when she just looked at him.

"I only have one working ovary thanks to a bout of endometriosis, and an extremely low rate of egg production. My chances of conceiving naturally are slim."

"Slim, but still a possibility," Dan clarified.

She stood up. "You can relax Dan, I'm not pregnant. I had a mild vision, that's all."

Dan stood toe to toe with her and placed his hands on either side of her face. "Still, the point's been raised. It may be difficult for you to conceive, but not impossible. As appealing as the thought of having my child growing inside of you is, now is not the time. We'll need to be careful."

A tear escaped, despite her best efforts to hold it back.

"When we have Bree back in your arms we'll spend some time discussing giving her a little brother or sister."

Rebecca collapsed against his chest. The thought of holding Bree again is all that kept her going some days. It would be so easy to tumble over the edge, into a pool of self-pity. "Don't get your hopes up. The odds aren't in my favor."

"For now, we'll be more careful, just in case your body decides to throw you a curve ball. Hey." But he smiled as she wiped her eyes with the edge of his T-shirt. He swung an arm around her shoulder and aimed them toward the stairs. "Let's get you to bed."

# Chapter Fourteen

No cars stood in the driveway of Pete's apartment. No one seemed to be home on the main floor, or on the upper level of the house where the other tenant lived. Not surprising, in the middle of the day, but it gave Dan something to do while he waited to hear from Ryker.

Despite his bragging, Ryker had yet to get back to Dan with his report on Pete. Not a good sign.

Dan headed around front to where Rebecca waited by the car when he got the text. "Shit." He rubbed shaking hands over his face, while he leaned back against the brick wall. He knew, damn it. Hell, he knew three years ago, but didn't listen to his gut. How the hell did he tell the woman he loved he fucked up? That because of his colossal screw up, she might never see her daughter again.

Rebecca came around the corner, cellphone in hand. "He's still not answering his phone, and he didn't show up for work today. What about you?"

"Nothing." He averted his eyes as he tucked his phone into the back pocket of his jeans. "The door's locked, and there's no sign of forced entry. From what I can see through the window there's no sign of a struggle inside either. If someone grabbed him, it must have been from somewhere else. I'll run his plates, see if his car's been seen anywhere." He started walking around to the front.

"We should stop by Ruby's and ask," Rebecca said, following along behind him. "She manages to be on top of everything that happens around here. Besides, it's almost lunchtime and I'm hungry."

"I think I'll have the chief run Pete's plates," Dan said ignoring the questions in her eyes once in the car. She'd have plenty more questions when he told her what Ryker found. "I'd rather just go back to the house." He started the engine. "We can eat there."

"Sure, no problem," Rebecca agreed.

She suspected something, he knew it by the way she let him have his way without arguing. Saw it in the way she bit her bottom lip to keep herself from asking straight out what his problem was.

Christ, her compassionate silence on the ride home only drove the knife deeper. Getting out of the car, he palmed the keys to the house she trusted him with, went straight back to the kitchen, found the bottle of beer tucked way to the back of the bottom shelf, twisted the cap off and chugged it. Maybe he'd be the one to knock her off the wagon with one vicious shove. Hell, it couldn't get much worse.

"Okay then." Rebecca tossed her purse on the table and faced him, hands on hips. "I don't know why, but you're in a pissy mood. I get it, I have them sometimes myself." She walked the few remaining steps to him and rammed her finger into his chest. "But when I do, I try my best not to take them out on the people I'm with." He took another sip of beer while he grappled with a way to tear her world apart. Her finger moved to tap her own chest. "Have I done something to set you off?"

He took a gulp this time. "No."

"If you don't stop hiding behind that beer and start talking to me right now, I swear to god I'll smash the damn bottle over your bloody head."

And he deserved it. A deep sigh escaped him. He turned away from her and set the empty bottle down on the counter. He gripped the beige Formica until the sharp edge dug into his hands. Through the window, he saw the swing-set Rebecca set up for Bree in the back yard. The empty seat mocked him as it swayed back and forth in the breeze. He swallowed past the lump in his throat and turned. It might soon be time to face his demons, but he needed to face Rebecca first.

Her face held no color, and thin lines bracketed her mouth. She wore her fear like a shield, inviting him to throw everything he had at her. This might prove to be the blow that cracked the hard shell she donned every morning.

Dan forged in. "Ryker sent me his report." Her eyes widened, and her breathing quickened. "He confirmed something. Something I suspected long ago." He scrubbed both hands over his face, not wanting to see her pain. When he lowered his hands, her worried eyes stared back at him. "Pete Hayes doesn't exist."

"What are you talking about? We were married. As much as I like to think so, he isn't a figment of my imagination." Rebecca threw her hands up. "You grilled us both for hours when Bree disappeared."

92

"Peter Hayes doesn't exist," he repeated. "It's an alias."

A hint of panic flashed in Rebecca's eyes before she crossed over to complete denial. "That's not true. I've seen his driver's license, his credit cards. Our marriage license for god's sake. I know who I married."

"They're all fakes."

"What about his passport, Dan? He just renewed it last year when he flew to Germany on business. I know because I ran into him at the dentist. He stopped in to ask the dentist to sign the application. After nine-eleven, security is tight. It must be damn near impossible for someone to get a fake passport."

"Difficult, but not impossible."

"This is Pete we're talking about here. He's not that smart. He certainly doesn't have the connections it would take to pull off a stunt like this."

Dan put his hands on her shoulders. She shrugged them off and started pacing. "This is insane." He could see her consider every possible scenario. "Oh my God." Her hands flew to her mouth. "Is he in the witness protection program?"

She wasn't quite there yet, but Dan knew it wouldn't be long now. At the moment, he could tell she didn't want comfort from him, but she'd need it soon. He needed her to let him in again.

"He's not a protected witness."

"Then what the hell is he?" she yelled. "Tell me what would make a man fake his entire identity? Is he a bigamist? An ex-con? A child molester? Tell me, damn it."

There. Her light bulb moment. Her eyes widened as the blood drained from her face. He got to her just as her knees gave out.

Dan carried her up to her room and gently laid her on the bed. He placed the blame for this squarely where it belonged. He'd made the mistake of trusting a friend. That misplaced trust cost Rebecca her daughter. Her hair fell across her face and he brushed it away, marveling at the depth of his feelings. He never intended to fall in love with her. It wasn't the first time he'd been drawn in one direction, while common sense sent him elsewhere. His body responded to her, even back when they first met, but he never acted on it, not until the night he left. She'd been married, for God's sake, however unhappy that marriage turned out to be. And part of a case. It hadn't done much to stop him.

He went into the bathroom, looked in the medicine cabinet, and found the nearly full bottle of Zoplicone. The expiration date passed a month ago, but he'd take his chances. He sat on the edge of the bed and lifted the decanter of water she kept on the bedside table. Upending the lid, he filled it, and placed two of the small blue tablets next to it. Then he waited.

It wouldn't be long now. Her eyes swished back and forth beneath paper-thin covers. A soft whimper escaped her lips, but she pressed them together, as though stopping the sound would stop the pain. Tears leaked from beneath her lashes before consciousness fully returned. When her eyes flipped open, the horror of her nightmare stared out at him.

Dan watched her struggle to remember. Felt her revulsion as the scene played out in her head. Could practically see her mind dip behind a wall of defense and crumble under the weight of her pain. His gaze followed the trail of tears. Watched them detour around her ear, before trickling down past the crease of her neck and sink into the pillow beneath her head.

Other than opening her eyes, she didn't move. Taking her limp hand in his, he offered comfort he wasn't sure she even recognized.

Her mouth opened, but no sound came out. He leaned forward in alarm when her face turned blue. She gasped, and then sucked in a great gulp of air, which rode out on a keening wail that coasted forever. She rolled away from him and curled into a fetal position. Dan said nothing, just rubbed her back, and occasionally wiped the moisture dripping from her nose.

Her voice, when it finally emerged, sounded hoarse and dry, "Go away."

"Here, drink some of this," he said gently and leaned over to roll her shoulder down to the bed and turn her toward him.

She rolled onto her back, brought her arm up, and swiped the snot from beneath her nose with the back of her hand. "Leave me alone."

Dan wedged his arm beneath her shoulders and lifted her up high enough to take a sip of water. Her tongue flicked out to lick at the droplets left on her lips. He pressed the glass against them again, letting her drink.

"Here you go babe, take this." He slipped the pills between her lips. "Drink up." She drank again, and he checked her mouth to make sure the pills went down.

"Don't call me babe." She rolled over again the moment he lowered her shoulders to the bed. "Oh God, I need my baby," she cried.

Dan rubbed her back and waited for the meds to kick in. "I know, I know," he lied, not knowing anything at all.

# Chapter Fifteen

Rebecca took a deep breath and prepared herself for the confrontation with Dan. She headed for the stairs, stopping at the open door to her home office when she noticed the sofa, made up into a bed. Good, that saves her the trouble of explaining where things stood. She found him working at the dining room table, two cups of coffee at his elbow.

Rebecca took the mug he handed her, needing the hit of caffeine too much to care who it came from. She mumbled her thanks and continued into the kitchen.

Dan followed and leaned against the doorframe, waiting. With a small shake of his head at her obstinate silence, he turned and went back to his computer. How long she could keep this up, she didn't know. She was never very good at playing the silent game, even as a kid. Oh, she could hold a grudge, but keeping quiet about it was where she ran into problems. It became one of the petty things she did to annoy Pete toward the end.

Pete. God, she'd been so wrong about him. Questions tumbled through her mind. Dan better be prepared to answer them, now that the damn drugs were out of her system. She needed more information. What part did Pete play in Bree's disappearance? Why? What the hell has he done with her? She'd lain in bed a long time that morning thinking it through. It didn't add up.

Rage bubbled to the surface, followed by fear and shame, much like the day she first went to Dan for help. But she couldn't help Bree by throwing a temper tantrum. "Dan?"

He appeared in the doorway a moment later. "Ready to talk now?" At her curt nod, he pulled out the chair opposite her and sat down.

Rebecca fired the first shot, "You've got nerve, I'll give you that. Your attitude is putting me on the defensive. I don't like it. I'm not the one who lied here."

Dan's eyes never wavered from hers. "Fair enough," he conceded. "I'm only trying to give you space, not gain the upper hand."

"I need the truth Dan."

Dan placed a thick folder on the table, opened it, and spun it around so Rebecca could read it. She sucked in her breath. Sabrina's pre-school picture, the one Rebecca had given the police three years ago, stared back at her.

"This is the case file the FBI has on Sabrina. Every interview, every lead, every thought our investigators had is in there." He paused, until she looked up from Bree's face. "I promise you, there'll be no more secrets. Not from me."

Saying nothing, Rebecca started turning pages, reading report after report. Most of it she knew, she'd lived it. A few offhand comments, reflections really, from some of the agents surprised her, and she read those aloud, asking for clarification.

"Rebecca and Peter Hayes are presenting a united front on the surface, but the marriage is in trouble. Apparently I didn't do such a good job of hiding the true state of my marriage after all."

Rebecca read on. "Peter Hayes often takes vacations alone, under the guise of business travel. Look into possible affair." That one shook her. She never suspected Pete of cheating on her. Her eyes scanned the page to check for a name, but couldn't find one. "Did you ever find out the name of the woman having an affair with Pete?"

Dan shook his head, and his eyes dueled with hers, looking for answers she wasn't ready to give. "We knew the two of you were shaky at best, but found nothing to substantiate an affair, by either of you."

Rebecca raised her brows before she continued reading. She asked a question now and then, and received an answer, but made no further effort to engage him in conversation.

She closed the file. "I don't see anything in here about Pete's assumed identity. I thought you promised no more secrets?"

Dan got up and placed his mug in the sink. "That never made it into the case file."

"Clearly." Her face tightened. "Why not? Everything else did. Even the tiniest speculation got written down. Tell me, why didn't this particular idea get noted and followed up on?"

She could see the vein in Dan's temple pulse. "The agent responsible for looking into Pete's past—"

"The agent responsible? When it's your team, you're the agent responsible."

"Agent Dawes," Dan bit out, "mentioned Pete's squeaky clean record in an offhand comment during lunch one day. Usually squeaky-clean raises red flags with me. Everyone wishes for a do-over moment at least once in his life, a decision or action he'd take back, given the chance. Pete had none. With the exception of his marriage, his life followed his carefully laid out plan, up to that point."

Rebecca cringed at the memory of her eagerness to live her dream. She'd been such a doormat. "Why aren't agent Dawes' notes and your suspicions on record?"

Something flickered behind Dan's eyes, but disappeared too quickly for her to put a name to it.

"We had a brief conversation during a very hectic time. It didn't make it into any of his reports, and it should have, you're right. Once we moved the investigation back to the field office, I had a chance to read the files in more depth. By that point, we already eliminated both of you as possible suspects. You each had solid alibis, Pete at work, and you visiting with your neighbor while Sabrina attended preschool. I focused my attention on finding Sabrina. NATs, new agent trainees," he clarified at her look of confusion, "make rookie mistakes all the time. I let this one slide. I screwed up Rebecca. If not for me, Sabrina might be here right now."

"You believe Pete played a role in Sabrina's disappearance. What role?" Rebecca kept her focus on the questions, not ready to follow where they led quite yet.

"We haven't figured that out yet, but we strongly suspect his involvement."

"Parents who abduct their children disappear with them. That didn't happen."

"Chief Bains has men at Pete's apartment now, looking for trace evidence. But you're right. If a father intends to raise his child, he'd obtain alternate identities, and go off somewhere to do just that. The fact that Pete's maintained his life here threw suspicion off him."

"What other intent would a father have?" The words left her mouth before she could stop them. She already knew the answer. She'd spent

98

the last twenty four hours reliving that nightmare.

"We're looking at Pete again, combing through his life. Soon we'll discover everything he never wanted us to know. Ryker's been on it all night. He'll find something, trust me." Dan winced.

"Everyone's entitled to a mistake, but you have to admit, this is a big one. One deliberately kept from me. That's the part I can't forgive. I'll continue living this lie for Bree's sake, but things will have to change." The tightening of his jaw told her he knew what she meant.

"I'm not giving up this time Rebecca. I won't leave here until Sabrina comes home. Trust in that, at least."

"It's the only reason you're still here."

# Chapter Sixteen

Rebecca kept her silence on the drive into town with Dan. Bains hadn't said much beyond asking her to come down to the precinct. Now, unease rippled through her as she sat on one of two brown metal folding chairs across the table from where he sat. Her eyes avoided the mirror at the far end of the room.

"What's happened? Have you found another body? Bree?"

Bains cleared his throat and licked his lips. Rebecca struggled to place the officer standing beside him. Turner, she remembered, from the hit and run.

"Rebecca?" Bains' voice brought her focus back to him. "You look a little unwell, are you all right?"

Her hands went to her temples as she nodded. "There must have been more of the drug left in my system than I thought."

"What drug would that be?"

"Rebecca hasn't been sleeping well. Last night I convinced her to take a couple sleeping pills."

"It would be best if you let Rebecca answer my questions on her own."

Dan's lips thinned, but he nodded.

Turner took a notebook from his pocket and jotted something down. "Why did you feel the need to take sleeping pills last night?" Bains asked.

"I've been under a little stress." Rebecca winced, hearing the snap in her voice. Bains waited patiently, making Rebecca regret her tone even more. She looked to Dan, wondering how much to say, but he kept his expression neutral. "What's all this about?"

"When did you last see Pete?"

"Pete? I don't run into him very often, why?"

"Did you run into him this past Sunday?"

Rebecca gnawed on her lower lip. "I saw Pete at Ruby's when I stopped in to pick up breakfast, yes." She couldn't look at Dan. She'd pitched the muffins long before finally getting home.

"Did you talk to him?"

Bains knew she had, of course. Hell, there were a dozen witnesses to her attack on Pete. Not one of her best moments. She swallowed. "Argued might be more accurate."

"What did you argue about?"

Rebecca's eyes flicked to Dan's stony expression before turning back to Bains. "I called him a heartless bastard who didn't care about anyone, never mind his own daughter." She lifted one brow. "He disagreed."

Dan leaned forward in his chair, but a look from Bains halted him.

"Is that all that happened?"

"He pushed my buttons, okay? I'm not proud of the way I reacted, but I'd had a rough week. He suggested I get therapy for my anger issues." She bared her teeth in a weak attempt at a smile. "Apparently there's a time limit for a parent to mourn her missing child, and my time is up. He acted like he didn't care. No, he really didn't give a damn." She shrugged. "I lost my temper."

"Did you make any physical contact with Pete during this altercation?"

"Don't tell me he's pressing charges for a little shove for God's sake. He barely moved."

"What happened after you shoved Pete?" Turner's hand hovered over the notebook as Bains spoke, but he didn't write anything down. They already knew the answers.

"Nothing. Pete said something about me needing help. Then he left."

"Pete left first then?"

Rebecca looked over at Dan, who shifted his chair a hair closer to hers. "Yes. I'll apologize if I have to. Will that make Pete happy?" Bains gave her a pained grimace. She didn't think it had anything to do with the cast on his arm.

"I don't know what will make Pete happy. No one's seen him since he left the diner."

A flicker of alarm shot through her. "He's probably out of town on business again."

Bains shook his head. "We've checked. His car's been abandoned, over by Wilmott Creek."

"Kids going joy riding again? No, that makes no sense."

"Can you account for your whereabouts on Sunday morning, Mr. Cooper?"

"I awoke alone at Rebecca's house, at eight thirty. I had a conference call with two associates that lasted about an hour. From about eleven to noon I would guess." Dan recited Evan and Ryker's contact information to Turner. "I used the land line at the house."

"Had Rebecca returned home at this point?"

"She came in a couple of hours later, around two."

Bains turned back to Rebecca. "You left Ruby's just after nine thirty. Where did you go from there?"

"Nowhere in particular." The flicker of alarm Rebecca felt earlier rang full blast now. "I just drove around for a while, trying to clear my head."

"Three and a half hours is a long time to calm down. You must have been pretty angry."

"Chief—" Dan stood up.

"Can you be more specific about where you went?"

"I drove around town for a bit, and then headed for the park. It's a quiet place to think."

"Did you see Pete again after you left Ruby's?"

"No. He'd already driven away when I came out."

"Can you explain how your prints came to be on his driver's side window? We found a receipt for the car wash from Saturday, so they would have to have been left sometime after that."

"I...I looked in his car when I got to Ruby's. I must have put my hand on the glass when I bent over."

"What about this?" Bains reached out and took an evidence bag from Officer Turner. He held it up for her to see.

Rebecca's teeth worried at her lip again. The bag held a tube of Marshall's Botanical Lip Balm, just like the ones she buys. The natural medicinal properties helped heal the damage caused from biting her lips all the time.

"Is this yours?"

"I use one like that but mine's in my purse." Rebecca picked up the bag she placed on the floor earlier. She reached into the open pouch on the front, but her hand came up empty. "I don't understand. I always keep it here, in easy reach since I use it so often." She rummaged around the main compartment, and then dumped the contents onto the table. No lip balm fell out.

"We'll check to see if your prints are on this one just to be sure. Where do you buy these?" Bains continued.

"I order them online, or drive into Phoenix. They don't sell them in stores around here."

He smiled. "That sounds a bit inconvenient. You must get several at a time."

"Of course I—"

Dan put a hand on her shoulder. "Don't say anything more."

Bains sent a wry look in Dan's direction, and then faced Rebecca again. "When you looked into Pete's car window did you see anything unusual?"

"Just a DVD case on the seat and a lot of garbage."

"You didn't see any blood?"

Dan moved behind Rebecca and placed both hands on her shoulders now.

"You think something happened to Pete and you think I did it," Rebecca whispered.

Officer Turner stepped forward, cuffs in hand.

"This is weak Bains," Dan bit out. "You've got nothing that places Rebecca with Pete after he left Ruby's."

"It's enough. I'm sorry."

Rebecca glared at Dan while Officer Turner cuffed her. A sharp pain pinched between her shoulder blades when Turner pulled her arms behind her. It might not be rational to blame Dan, as well, for this, but too damn bad.

Dan spoke to Bains, but she heard nothing over the monotone voice of the officer behind her, reciting the Miranda rights.

\* \* \* \*

Rebecca shook her attorney's hand before heading down the front steps of the courthouse. Cooper leaned against the side of his car, arms folded across his chest, waiting. The two men watched Rebecca veer right, away from him, saw Cooper's hand reach out and grab her arm.

The finger she jabbed into his chest and the frown that followed her steps marching around the corner spoke louder than the words they were too far away to hear.

"You said the lip balm would provide enough evidence to make an arrest."

"And it did, but now it's missing from the evidence locker."

"A curious thing, that."

"I'm looking into it. We've got enough to question her, but not hold her. Not without the lip balm. The big shot lawyer Cooper brought in made sure we knew it, too. Not that she looks particularly grateful to him."

"We need her out of our way. I am running out of options. And time."

"Understood." He turned and walked down the hallway, nodding and smiling at people as he passed.

# Chapter Seventeen

Dan looked up from his laptop to watch Rebecca cross the dining room for the fourth time in two minutes. Frustration punctuated each step. He knew the lack of progress ate at her. She didn't need to hear a lecture on the virtues of patience. He went back to work when she picked up the overflowing basket of mail and started sorting through it, allocating each piece to what Dan recognized as read, action, and discard piles. He watched this routine before. It should keep her occupied for at least thirty minutes. Maybe he'd have something they could run with by then.

"Dan?"

The urgency in her voice brought him to her side. "What is it?"

"I think it's a warning." The crease on her forehead deepened. "Or a clue. I'm not sure."

Dan reached for a tissue from the box on the table and carefully retrieved the letter and envelope from Rebecca's hands. He laid them out on the coffee table. "I'm sending this to you at great risk to my family." He read the shaky handwriting. "I can't do this again. I refuse to sacrifice another child for something I no longer believe in. He is very convincing, charismatic even. I believed in his prophesy, we all did. We were raised to. He is an evil man interested only in increasing his own power. The rest of us are a necessary convenience, delivering his precious vessels. But power comes at a price, one I'm no longer willing to pay. You've paid a price too Rebecca, one you will forfeit on September twelfth without knowing the reason. You deserve to understand why your child was stolen from you and why she will die. She is a chosen one." Dan looked up and saw despair fill Rebecca's eyes.

Her nails dug into his forearm. "September twelfth is Bree's birthday," she whispered. "That's—" Her hand flew to her mouth.

"Ten days from now," Dan finished. "Christ. Who is this from?" He flipped the envelope over with a pen but found the back blank. "The post mark says Phoenix, but that doesn't mean much. Someone else could have posted it. Even if the sender posted it themselves, they'd be long gone by now." Fear would carry them far and quickly. He looked down and continued reading. The handwriting scrawled across the page now, barely legible. "He's coming, I have to go. It's up to you to stop this Rebecca."

"We need to get these sealed and analyzed. Do you have plastic baggies?" While Rebecca went to the kitchen, Dan gingerly picked up the envelope again. Something felt off. He tapped the envelope against the table until a picture slid out. He studied the photo of Rebecca standing behind a table displaying what looked like preserves. "Can you tell me anything about this picture? Who took it? When?" he asked. He slipped it into a baggie before holding it up.

"Let me see."

Dan leaned in and held it closer to her. "Two years ago, the first week of April to be exact, at the Pinal County fair."

"You seem pretty sure of the date."

The fair is held every year about the same time." Rebecca pointed to the background display. "See that sign there? Ruby's Jams and Preserves? I painted it. She only used it the one year."

"Why?"

"They expanded their product line to include pies, and I did a new sign for the following year."

"They?" Dan pressed. "Ruby and who? There's no other name on the sign."

"Carrie. Ruby started out alone at first, but now they run it together. The fair's been running five years now, but that's the first year I got involved.

"Why would she send you this picture?"

"She?"

Dan sat down and laid the picture on the coffee table again. "The handwriting, the phrasing, and the way she wants to make sure you understand. She describes the leader of this," Dan searched for the right word. "Cult, as charismatic. It's written by a woman, I'm sure of it. But who? Do you remember who took this picture?"

"God, no. It could have been anyone. Ruby worked at the diner that morning and wanted the afternoon shift at the booth instead. They asked me to come in and help for a bit. I arrived around eleven, and it wasn't long after that I had to leave. I remember feeling bad that I couldn't stay longer."

"Tell me about the animals."

"They have livestock shows, but the big attractions, at least for the little ones, are the pony rides and petting zoo. They were set up right behind our booth." She sat beside Dan and leaned over to examine the photo again. "These people here," Rebecca tapped her nail on the picture, "are in line for the pony rides."

"Do you recognize any of them? I realize the image is small. I'll scan it and enlarge it later."

Rebecca shook her head. "I'm sorry, I don't recognize anyone. The fair draws people from all over the County." He saw anxiety creep in and threaten to overtake her. "We only have ten days." Her eyes closed. "Less than ten days to find Bree."

Dan pulled out his phone and pressed a number on speed dial. "Ryker, we have new information. I'm sending you an image, a picture mailed to Rebecca. I need you to dissect it." He filled Ryker in. "I need to find out what's in the picture that someone wants Rebecca to know, and I need it now. Thanks pal, I owe you."

Dan wanted to wrap his arms around Rebecca and absorb some of her pain. He cupped her shoulders, but she shrugged even that small comfort off and left. He watched her battle from a forced distance. She pulled down the bottle of wine she insisted on keeping in a cubby next to the pantry and stared at it for a full minute. Her hand shook when she returned the bottle to the shelf. He couldn't fight this demon for her, no matter how much he might want to. Dan retreated behind his computer and prepared the file to send to Ryker.

He let the letter play through his mind again. He jotted down the words and phrases that tugged at him.

*Sacrifice.*

*Precious vessels.*

*I believed in his prophesy.*

*We were raised to.*

He read the last one again. "I believed in his prophesy, we all did. We were raised to." Dan leaned back in his chair and let his thoughts flow. One man, a prophet, able to coerce others to bring him children.

Their own children?

*Sacrifice.* She couldn't sacrifice another child. A mother of at least two children, who's given up a child before to this cause. Whose mother is this? Nicole's? Jennifer's. A child they'd yet to discover?

He leaned back again continuing his analysis. What payout did the sacrifice bring? Power. He increased his own power. But what of the others? What could compel so many to do the unthinkable? What is the prophesy's premise? Its promise? To whom? How many were part of the group? For how long?

*We were raised to.* He kept coming back to that. Parents raising children as members. Dan jotted down another note. *Generations. Age span of members extensive.*

Why the loss of belief? Because she can't bear to give up another child. They die on their birthday. Why? Coming full circle? No, they die at the age of seven. Dan wrote down *7 – reflects perfection—talk to Kaden.* She is a chosen one. The hair on his arms stood up. Chosen how, he wrote. *What makes these children special?*

"Shit." He pulled out his phone. He'd need the whole damn team to bring these assholes down.

# Chapter Eighteen

The entire team gathered in Rebecca's living room six hours later. Kaden, the sole team member Rebecca had yet to meet, slipped in quietly, and settled in among the others with little fanfare. Finn, the last to arrive, came straight over to Rebecca. Dan bit back a curse when Finn grabbed both her shoulders and leaned down to place a gentle kiss on her cheek.

"We'll be getting your baby back for you Rebecca. Don't you be worrying about a thing now." Finn moved to stand behind the chair Kaden sat in, reaching over to ruffle her short dark hair. She reached up and grabbed his fingers, twisting until Finn went down to his knees with a yelp of pain. "Have mercy woman. You're always picking on me."

Dan reached around, pulled a stack of papers off the dining room table behind him, and passed them around. "You haven't had much time to review the email I sent with the letter and picture. Ryker enlarged the photo and digitally enhanced it. Take a look." Dan handed Rebecca a copy. "Do you see anyone you recognize in the lineup?"

She studied the photo. Ryker had done an excellent job of enhancing the background images, but Rebecca shook her head. "Still nothing. I don't get it. Why send a clue we can't decipher?"

"She was clearly under pressure when she wrote the letter. Maybe she just grabbed something handy that fit," Nick offered.

"I may have something here." Ryker shifted his laptop so they could see the screen. "I enhanced the faces of the four children in line. It's grainy, but it's enough to run them through facial recognition software and the missing children data base."

"You got a hit with missing persons?" Finn asked, surprise stamped on his face.

"Not exactly." Ryker turned the computer around again and hit a few keys. "When I didn't get a hit with MP I dug a little deeper." He patted the top of his laptop, like he would a loyal dog. "I sent Bella here on a hunt for any reports filed with the police or CPS involving young girls."

Dan grimaced. "That would make for a long list."

"Yeah, well, factoring in the time frame, hair, age, and vicinity helped narrow it some. Bella is very thorough." He hit a few more keys then spun the laptop around again. It showed a split screen this time. One of the kids from the pony ride line on one side, and on the other, about a year older, maybe four, a picture of the same girl, curly brown hair framing a freckled face wearing a ghost of a smile. Sad eyes looked out at them. "Meet Emily Banks."

Dan bent over to get a closer look. "When did the missing person report come in?

"It didn't."

"So we've identified a child who isn't missing. At least that narrows the field down a bit." Dammit. They needed that lead.

Ryker shook his head. "You don't understand. Three years ago, Brad and Nora Banks lived in Salt Lake City, Utah with their lovely daughter Emily. A year and a half later Brad got a promotion at work and they moved to Texas. Or at least that's the story they told their neighbors."

"What really happened?" Nick asked.

"They disappeared."

"All of them?" Rebecca gasped.

"Wait a minute, how do you know this if no MP report exists?" Evan asked.

"That would be where Miss Myrna Fielding, spinster, comes in."

"Myrna who?" Finn scratched his chin.

"Myrna Fielding went to Colorado to visit her brother, Chester."

Nick choked back a laugh. "Chester Fielding? You've got to be kidding me."

"Trust me. I couldn't make this stuff up." Ryker rolled his eyes. "Miss Myrna decided to treat Chester to his favorite ice cream at the local parlor. Who did she see there but Brad and Nora Banks. The thing is, they're not Brad and Nora Banks anymore."

"Is anyone else completely lost here?" Finn helped himself to a cookie from the plate on the table.

"I'm heading in that direction Finn." Evan's gaze settled on Ryker. "What happened when Miss Myrna confronted Brad and Nora?"

"She didn't. She took her brother down the street for fudge instead and grilled him about the Banks'." He looked up, suddenly serious. "The childless Banks' as it turns out."

"Let me get this straight," Dan interrupted. "One day Brad, Nora and Emily Banks are living as one big happy family in Salt Lake City. The next, Emily is gone, and Brad and Nora are living under new names in a new state and without a child. Is that right so far?"

Ryker nodded.

"And no missing person report or death certificate has ever been filed for Emily?" Dan clarified.

Ryker nodded again. "When Miss Myrna recognized them as the same couple from her building complex she went to the police. They were short staffed, and the officer on desk duty worked a double to allow all available personnel to work an accident scene. A school bus was involved in a multi-car pile-up on I-70 with fatalities. It was a mess. Six children and the bus driver died. Of course, the drunk driver who caused the fiasco walked away without injury. In the chaos of the day, somehow the report never got logged. In fact, it went missing, until a renovation last month. Officers are just getting around to looking at the report now. It hasn't been established as an MP yet. It's just an allegation by a citizen that needs following up on. Sadly, the police figure if a child is genuinely missing, the parents are going to report it. Or neighbors or schools will. Even if the parents were guilty of foul play, they'd need to make the report to cover their tracks. The police have their hands full with legitimate missing children. This allegation is on their list, but it's a long way down."

Dan watched Ryker take in the astonished faces in the room.

"Like I said, I couldn't make this stuff up if I tried." Ryker gestured to Kaden. "Evan sent Kaden to Oklahoma City yesterday on a different case, and asked her to head over to Colorado to verify the story. After a quick recon and search of the home, she found no sign that a child ever lived in that house. Not even a picture in the family photo albums. It all checks out."

Evan looked around the room, his gaze hesitating on each picture of Sabrina placed throughout. He cleared his throat. "It takes a cold heart to raise a child for three years, and then completely erase her from your life.

They didn't keep any photos, which mean they're careful. Let's say, for the sake of argument, that Brad and Nora Banks are part of this. It follows that Emily could be with Bree. The replacement child, if you like. If Bree is—I mean goes—well, shit."

"I believe the word you're looking for is murdered, or perhaps killed or sacrificed. Take your pick," Rebecca interrupted, her face white.

"If things go as planned, and we're here to make sure it doesn't," he emphasized, "they'll need a replacement for Sabrina. This kind of plan doesn't fall into place overnight. Many things had to happen over a long stretch of time to have the child ready for hand-off now."

"Mrs. Reynolds sent me the picture," Rebecca blurted out.

Dan stood and started pacing. "Of course, it makes perfect sense. According to the letter, she's done this before. She knows you, which accounts for the familiar way she addresses you, and the guilt she feels. They disappeared, on the run it seems. We assumed their cohorts tipped them off that we were on to them. The timing of that might be a coincidence. The date to hand their child over is closing in. Maybe someone contacted them, asked them to bring her in. If the Reynolds had a reason to make a run for it that would be the catalyst."

Dan ached to comfort Rebecca, but that wouldn't be happening. He looked over to where she stood on the opposite side of the room, biting her lip. As far away from him as she could get, physically and emotionally. Uneasy looks passed among the team. Thank God, they were too polite to ask questions.

"I'd like to talk about the letter now," Evan continued. "We're beginning to get a picture of how this group works." He picked up the printout Dan handed out earlier. "Disturbing messages are written between the lines of this letter. Talk of sacrifice, prophets, it all adds up to cult activity. Usually based on religion, but not always. The number seven is significant." Evan nodded to Kaden.

"Right. The number seven has great meaning and power in many cultures," Kaden began, "seven cosmic stages, seven heavens, seven chakras of the body, and seven circles of the Universe. Seven represents completeness and totality, perfection and reintegration, among other things. The seventh ray of the sun is the path humans use to pass from this world to the next. In magic, cords are knotted seven times for spellbinding. Take your pick. For our purposes, I think these next two might be closer to where our perps are coming from. In Buddhism, seven is the number of ascent, or of ascending to the highest. Hebrews believe seven is the number of occult intelligence."

Kaden looked around the group. "If the purpose is to sacrifice the perfection of an innocent child, a state believed to be achieved at the age of seven, by the way; it could be this ascent to the highest that's the payoff. One would have to assume this pinnacle, once achieved, gave the bearer a certain amount of power, be it physical or spiritual. Clearly these sociopaths have taken whatever belief they chose to cast off from and warped it into something that better suits their needs."

"Any further reports from our last meeting?" Dan asked the group.

"Brindle's isn't the dead end it first appeared to be," Ryker stated. "Ridgeway's exaggerated standard of living can be attributed to a rich sugar daddy—or mommy in this case. If this group is filtering the children through the agency, they're doing it under Ridgeway's radar. At least up to now. I believe something made her suspicious. Ridgeway did a little digging of her own. Her office computer shows a recent search of her partner, Karen Chambers', financial records, and family history." Ryker looked at Dan. "She also hired a new receptionist last week. I'm looking deeper into the agency's financials to see if there's any way Chambers has played with them."

"Evan got back to me on the trafficking angle. There's nothing there at the moment." Dan looked at Nick. "Any insights on why they always have two girls on hand?"

"I don't think there's anything specific about the number as it would apply here." He looked to Kaden for confirmation and at the shake of her head, continued, "They don't seem to go out of order, so having two isn't likely to be for back-up, in case one gets sick or is deemed inappropriate. Best guess is they space the abductions out to avoid detection. Hell, if some of these people aren't even reporting their children missing it could be a long time before anyone picks up on the pattern. We assumed that geography played a part. Since the Banks' lived in Utah, that widens the search area. There's no way to tell how long this has been going on."

"Which brings me to my thoughts on that matter." Dan swung a dining room chair around and straddled it. The woman who wrote the letter referred to being 'raised to believe.' To me, this suggests the cult's been active for years, maybe even generations."

Dan paused when Finn got up to stand next to Rebecca, who had her arms curled around her midriff and wobbled slightly.

Finn draped an arm around her shoulders. "We're getting closer to her. Don't lose heart now. We've gained a lot of ground here today."

Rebecca raised haunted eyes to his. "But we've also lost precious time."

# Chapter Nineteen

Joshua drove the motorcycle a mile past the empty parking lot at the Red Eye pay station, before heading off road for another quarter mile and stashing the bike. He grabbed his backpack and doubled back on foot, expecting the members to arrive soon. A quick look at his watch told him to hustle into place before then.

They called an unscheduled meeting, without inviting him. *No surprise there.* He acted stupid by showing defiance at the last gathering, he knew that.

He found it hard to believe his parents chose these people to guide him. When his parents died in a car accident two years ago, they left him two key items, the deed of ownership to the garage and a letter explaining his obligations to his extended family. He'd often suspected his parents of being involved in something sketchy, a pyramid scheme, or something similar. What else explained how his dad got enough money to buy the garage when he drank his paycheck every week? Never, in his darkest nightmare, had Joshua imagined this group of lunatics.

He spent a lot of time listening and keeping his mouth shut during his apprenticeship, learning from the outset to play along. Hell, it felt good to be a part of something bigger than him, to be honest. At first, he got a kick out of having people around him who gave a shit. He learned a lot in two years, more than he was comfortable knowing, which he suspected they were aware of. They had a way about them of finding things out.

He scrambled up the ridge over the opening to the cave, careful to brush out his tracks behind him. He did a quick sweep of the area, checking for signs of animal life, before getting into a comfortable position and turning off his headlamp.

They arrived en masse, a few minutes later, traipsing into the clearing with no regard for the noise they made. *Why should they?* Josh thought. *No-one is around for miles.* Park officials condemned this old back entrance to the mining tunnels years ago. They created new paths, redirecting the public to more hospitable trails and entrances, none the wiser.

A few of the collective stopped to put on their robes. He didn't blame them for not wanting to make the hike in their warm confines. Two held the hedge away from the opening while the others went in. One will expect to see the cavern prepared and everyone ready to start when he arrived.

Josh did a quick head count. He didn't expect Six and Eight, which only left their esteemed leader, and judging by the flashlight bobbing up and down in the distance, he'd be here soon. By the time One arrived, Two, the trusted sidekick, waited alone at the entrance.

"Bring me up to date." One puffed for breath after the long hike in, more than usual Joshua noted. His skin, pale in the harsh beam of the flashlight, glistened with sweat. Dark circles pooled under his eyes.

Two craned his neck to check the entrance of the cave. "Everyone's here, everyone who's supposed to be," he corrected.

One put his hand on Two's shoulder. "Any problems taking care of that situation?"

"It's done."

"Good man." One stepped back and waited for Two to move the hedge.

*What the hell were they up to?* Josh let sufficient time pass before he followed, placing his feet with care. The opening ritual ended just as Josh rounded the final turn in the cavern. He stopped on the edge of the shadows, well within hearing distance.

"Our allegiance to thee."

"Report, Two."

"We're still waiting on Rebecca to visit her doctor."

Several heads turned toward Five. "She's too caught up in searching for her daughter. Nothing I could say or do would convince her to take the time."

Josh saw terror flash across her face from where he stood. Rightly so. He knew all too well the wrath that befell those who disappointed One.

"I discovered new information." Panic gave her voice an edge. "Her visions are back, and she knows Three's involved."

"Did she say as much?" Two demanded.

Five laughed. "No, Rebecca doesn't even think I know about her visions. She must think I'm an idiot." Five cleared her throat. "A vision came during our visit. Oh, she tried to pass it off as something else and I played along. Of course, I know a vision when I see one. The interesting part is the way she connected Three to us, just blurted out his name. It made me wonder how? The only non-members who know are the children."

Five had their attention again.

"I believe they're trying to warn her. I've been experimenting and I think I might be able to send Rebecca a bogus vision or two, just enough to throw her off." She stared at One. "At the very least, I can block any future visions the children might send."

"You can do this?" One asked.

"I tried it on Rebecca the other night with a degree of success. With a little fine tuning, I know I can do this."

"That would go a long way to make up for not getting her into the doctor. Make it happen." One turned to the collective. "We will have to revisit the idea of bringing Rebecca in." He walked over to place a hand on his pulpit. "I want to discuss our Twelfth brother." A low mumble filled the space.

"He is young," Seven offered, ever the voice of reason, "and still questioning his new family. He has yet to undergo induction. He can't be expected to truly appreciate the gifts he is receiving until then." Several nodded their heads in agreement.

"He is not strong enough," Nine spat out. "His parents should never have been invited in. Were it not for the legacy of his grandfather, Twelve would never have been worthy of our notice. He has received no training. I knew the ways by the age of ten. It's been two years, and Twelve still questions One's authority."

"In this matter, I agree with Nine." Seven raised a hand to get them to hear him out. "I have seen Twelve interact with Rebecca. His attachment reveals weakness. I'm not sure I trust him to do what's necessary, for the good of the collective. We are dealing with an unusual set of circumstances, with no precedents set for such an occurrence. We are forging new ground." Seven's voice tightened as he spoke and now a cough overtook him. He drank deeply from the canteen passed to him, and wiped his mouth with the back of his hand. "I believe we should vote on what steps to take from here."

"Thank you Seven and Nine. You have both raised good points. I, too, have reservations and believe Twelve should be watched closely. I will think on this during the remainder of our gathering. What is next on the agenda?"

"We need to discuss succession," Eight called out. "Who will replace the McKenney child? Six and Eleven are gone, taking our successor with them. Time is running short, preparations are due to begin."

One looked to his second in command briefly and then nodded.

Two stepped forward, smiling. "Six and Eleven have been located, and the child is on her way to us now." The murmurings grew to a rumble, and One scattered another offering over the flames, wasting their meager supply to regain control.

Oh, that's gonna piss him off, Josh thought, knowing the supply could only be replenished at the next ceremony.

"Enough," One shouted. "All of the players are in place, and we are ready to proceed." He stepped behind the pulpit, something he rarely did at this stage of a meeting, using it for support. One hand disappeared into the folds of his robe and pulled out a handkerchief. He blotted his brow a few times before tucking the cloth back into his pocket. "This issue with Twelve concerns me. My instincts tell me he is capable of causing a dangerous interruption at this crucial stage of our plan." One paused for breath. "I would like to suggest escalating our time line by a few days."

Seven frowned. "The date is predetermined. Ascension can only occur at the prime time for the full power of absorption to be achieved."

"As you stated so eloquently earlier, these are unusual circumstances. We may have no option other than to alter our plans to avoid detection. I have been looking into Sabrina's birth for alternate dates. Her birth, in the seventh hour of the day, though not ideal, will fulfill the requirements of the ceremony."

Silence met his recommendation. From what Joshua understood of the process, this broke with tradition in a big way. One needed to move things ahead, but Josh didn't believe fear over him screwing things up had anything to do with it.

Three's voice broke the silence. "Although born on the twelfth of September, Sabrina came into the world four days late, making the seventh her expected due date.

The collective turned their attention to Three and missed the smug smile curling over One's lips.

The murmuring started up again. "That should be more than enough." Nine stepped forward again. "After all, the chosen ones are marked at conception. It's the gods' intent that matters."

One nodded. "Agreed. We voted previously to bring Rebecca in if we failed to confirm the markings. We have been questioning Twelve's loyalty. I would like to entrust this task to him as a test. If he meets the challenge to our satisfaction, we will meet again to discuss his future with the collective. If he fails," One paused to meet the eyes of each member of the group, "the usual consequence for disloyalty will apply."

Two pulled the black bag from his robe and began passing out the stones. "To a vote then."

"I vote to advance the ascension ceremony by four days, to the seventh day of September."

With the vote completed, all in favor, the group disbanded. Joshua used the noise of clean up to cover his movements and made his way back to his hiding spot above the cave entrance. The members filed out one by one, some pausing to remove their robes before heading along the path back to their cars.

Their leader and his right hand man had yet to exit, and Joshua cocked an ear for sounds of their approach. There. He heard the slow but steady footfalls. Finally, Two appeared, with One leaning heavily on his arm.

"You are growing weaker each day," Two addressed One. "Moving the ascension up is the right thing to do. You'll regain your strength once the girl's power is transferred to you."

"We cannot afford to move things any further. I need every ounce of her power. The markings will be completed by tomorrow." One took a deep breath. Josh heard it rattle in his chest from where he hid. *Something is seriously wrong with One. He's weak and trying to hide it from the rest of the group.*

Joshua likened them to a wolf pack in many ways, loyal above all, but predatory as well. Any sign of weakness provided an opportunity for an ambitious member to overthrow the leader. No one spoke of it, but Josh knew that One achieved his current position through those very means. Two might be next in line, but a smart man would put his money on Seven to make the next move.

"You truly believe she is the key?" Two removed his robe and placed it in the tote bag at his feet.

"The book states a chosen one, later in life, will either sustain us, or bring the wrath of the gods upon us. If she is a missed chosen one and is marked in the way of the others, it is too late to do anything about it. If no mark is found, she is expendable. Either way, she dies. But, should she bear the mark that matches that on the book's cover, it can mean only one thing. With her gifts and the enormous transfer of power that would ensue if she were to ascend, his eminence would be most generous in his appreciation. You and I are the only ones who need know this.

"Understood."

"Good. Once Twelve has completed his task, kill him. Make it look like Cooper did it, if you can. I do not want anything tying this back to us, or to have to explain to the collective why we did not follow procedure. "

Two picked up his bag and held his other arm out for One to lean on. "Consider it done."

# Chapter Twenty

Carrie sipped her beer, scrunching her face up at the bitter taste. She watched him approach from her chair in the shadows of the porch. "Hello Josh," she said and chuckled when he jumped.

"What's so important you called me out here in the middle of the damn night? You couldn't tell me this over the phone?"

"One wants you to bring Rebecca in."

He sighed. "Did he say when?"

She clicked her tongue at him. "Tomorrow. Bring her here."

He looked in the window. "One wants her here? With the kids?"

Her eyes narrowed as she gestured at him with the beer bottle. "I'll worry about the kids. You do what you're told."

"Got another one of those around."

Carrie waved her hand in the direction of the door. "In the fridge."

"I'm just gonna use the bathroom," Josh called through the kitchen window.

Carrie smiled. "Whatever." She set her bottle on the railing, walked down the steps, careful to skip the one that squeaked, and pulled the nail from her pocket. She stood by her chair again, hands tucked into the front pockets of her jeans when he came back out.

He gave her a curious look, and drained his beer in a few long swallows. "I suppose I should be going. Tomorrow's going to be busy as it is." He handed her the empty bottle. "Thanks for the scintillating conversation, as always Carrie."

She gave him the finger with her free hand. "Up yours Josh." She set the bottle on the railing and headed inside before he got his car started. She had one final job to do tonight. For that, she needed to visit those brats in the back room.

Carrie turned the light on. The glare from the bare bulb streamed down on three small bodies. "Wakey, wakey," she called out. Two sets of eyes squinted back at her. The youngest squeezed her eyes shut, as though blocking Carrie out would make her go away. Didn't matter, she didn't need to talk to that one anyway.

"I'm hungry, is it morning yet?"

Sabrina patted the third girl's back. "Not yet Emily, go back to sleep."

"Hello Sabrina." Carrie smiled.

Sabrina glared back at her, silent.

"Aren't you the caring little mother hen? What would these pathetic wimps do without you?"

Sabrina rubbed Emily's back when she stirred, but remained silent.

"Whatever." Carrie rolled her eyes. "You've been a very naughty girl Sabrina, sending mommy dearest messages." Sabrina stilled. Carrie watched for a flicker that would give her away. "Not that you know enough to cause problems." Carrie continued, leaning back against the wall and examining a fingernail. "You should thank us for all the drugs we give you. It makes the time go faster." She snickered. "I went over to your mom's the other night. The night you tried to send her a message. You should have seen her, doubled up in pain like that. Poor thing." Bingo. Carrie saw the spark of anxiety flare in Sabrina's eyes. "You didn't realize how much your mother would suffer when you forced your visions on her, did you?" Carrie shrugged. "Or maybe you did and just didn't care. It doesn't matter one way or the other to me."

Carrie walked closer as she spoke. Sabrina's eyes followed Carrie's hand as she reached up and batted at the chain suspended beneath the light bulb. They watched the chain's shadow creep back and forth across the ceiling, closing in on Sabrina as it slowed.

"You're lying."

Carrie spread both hands up and out in front of her. "Swear to god," she said, shaking her head. "The pain got so bad she blacked out." Carrie's smile widened as Sabrina's face whitened. "It's not like getting a normal vision you know. They even have a name for it. You're a psychic vampire." Carrie watched the little do-gooder wrestle with her conscience.

"I hate to tell you this, but your mom's not handling your death very well." She made a tsking sound in her cheek and dragged her nails along the wall, scraping over layers of faded wallpaper as she circled the room. "She started drinking." Carrie looked Sabrina in the eye. "A lot. Did you know she still has breakfast every Saturday morning at Ruby's?" Carrie laughed and slapped her hands on her thighs. "And get this—she even orders a plate for you as if you were joining her." Carrie twirled her finger near her temple and laughed. "Cookoo. Everyone in town thinks so. No one even listens to what she says anymore." Carrie's eyes sharpened. "So there's really no point trying to send her messages."

Sabrina pleated the blanket on the bed, over and under, over and under, saying nothing.

"I can demonstrate how it feels if you like."

Sabrina looked up at Carrie's words.

"I've learned this neat little trick. I can block messages. If you try to send your mother another one I'll stop it. And when I do, the pain will rebound back on the sender." Carrie pointed her finger at Sabrina. "That would be you sweetie, in case you're not following me." The two lumps hiding under the covers jumped when Carrie slapped her hand on the wall. "Stop the visions now you little vampire, and we'll go on the way we've been." Carrie leaned in until her breath stirred the bangs on Sabrina's forehead. "Cross me and you'll understand real pain, up close and personal, you got that?"

Over and under, over and under. The blanket pleated beneath her fingers, but Sabrina remained silent.

"I suggest you get some sleep dearie, you're heading to the caves in the morning. Your time has come."

# Chapter Twenty-One

Rebecca parked her car in front of Ruby's and waited for Dan and Finn as they pulled in a few spots over. They couldn't leave her alone at the house, but figured she'd be fine at Ruby's, with a slew of witnesses who could swear to seeing Rebecca having coffee, and not breaking into Pete's apartment. Dan got out and walked over to Rebecca.

"I don't like the way your car is stalling. You need to get that looked at."

"That dude won't be going far if he doesn't get that patched soon." Dan turned at Finn's words and saw him point to the nail in the front left tire of a Buick.

Rebecca took the pink wrapper off a piece of gum and popped it in her mouth. Dan had teased her about chewing bubble gum. She looked away, mourning the loss of the little things, like a shared smile over a private joke. "That's Josh's. If he's inside I'll let him know. Maybe I'll speak to him about my car then too," she added for Dan's benefit. "How long do you two expect to be?" She continued on, not giving them a chance to answer, "I'm still not sure what you think you'll find that Chief Bains didn't."

"We'll be looking at it with a different set of eyes," Finn added. "We have a better idea what Pete's been up to. Something as innocent as a crumpled grocery receipt in the garbage could offer up a clue. We know what we're looking for now."

"Besides, we can't be sure a cop isn't part of this. Or Bains for that matter," Dan added. "No one will ever know we were there."

"Then why can't I come with you? I know what would be out of place for Pete."

Dan met her eyes. "You lived with him for eight years and never clued in to his secret. You don't know Pete as well as you thought." Rebecca winced. He might be right, but she didn't have to like it, dammit. "We'll be back within the hour." Dan pointed at the door of Ruby's. "Stay put. Promise." His voice lowered, rumbling out of him when she didn't respond.

Rebecca fought the urge to take his hand and pull him close to her. She practically tripped over him every day. He seemed to always be close by, keeping an eye on her. She missed him, missed the closeness. She turned her head, blinking hard to stop the tears. Bree took priority, and any remaining feelings she held for Dan would have to move to the back of the line. "Fine. I'll see you in an hour." She jerked open the door to Ruby's, not bothering to wait for them to leave.

She glanced over in concern at the corner booth where Norman Parks sat, coughing. She continued to where Josh sat at the counter, staring into his coffee, and grabbed the stool next to him. "Hey there," she smiled. "Why so glum?" Josh spun on his stool to face her, nearly knocking over his coffee in the process. Rebecca grimaced. "Sorry, I didn't mean to startle you."

"That's all right." He yawned. "Excuse me. I didn't get much sleep last night and no amount of caffeine seems to be helping. What brings you into town today?"

"Just errands," she hedged, nervous fingers folding the gum wrapper, again and again. "Thought I'd stop in for a break and a piece of Key Lime pie. I'm glad I ran into you."

Josh took a sip of coffee. "What's up?"

"My car's been stalling a lot lately. I've been meaning to bring it in, but something always comes up."

Josh stared into his cup for a few seconds before answering. "I have some time to look at it now. Why don't you have Ruby pack that pie up? You can have your break over in my waiting room just as well as you can here." Josh threw some change on the counter and called Ruby over. Before she knew it Rebecca stood in the parking lot, take-out bag in hand.

"Why don't you start her up and I'll see what I can hear."

Rebecca set the bag on the passenger seat and turned the key. It failed on the first two attempts before finally catching. She rolled down the window. "That's what's been happening on and off for a while."

He placed his hands on the doorframe and leaned down. "Sounds like the starter. It shouldn't take long for me to hook it up to be sure. Pull it around to the back entrance, that bay is empty."

"Are you sure about this Josh? I don't want to put you out."

125

"Busy is good on a day like today." He smiled. "Helps keep me awake. I'll meet you over there."

Rebecca glanced at the crowds inside and thought about her promise to Dan. *To hell with it. It's not like I'm going to be alone.* Josh opened the bay door for her when she drove around back. He waved her in, and hand signaled where he wanted the car.

He pointed to the small waiting room on the other side of the garage. "Sit and enjoy your pie and coffee. I'll hook her up and see what's wrong. Back in a few." He disappeared around the corner, pulling the bay door down on his way.

Rebecca eyed the orange grease stained molded plastic chair in the empty waiting room. What the heck. She sat and pulled out the plastic container of pie and the fork and dug in. No wonder Ruby added her pies to the county fair booth, no one made them better. She mulled over the thought of picking up an entire pie to bring back to the house when something hit the back of her head. She hit the gray concrete floor, and fell into blackness before the scream passed her lips.

\* \* \* \*

Rebecca groaned. Her arms ached, pulled back, and tied behind her. The scratchy rope dug into her wrists. Her head throbbed. Hell, her entire body hurt. She winced when the car bounced over several ruts in the road, shaking lose a tear from beneath the blindfold. Damn it. How could she have been so stupid? The car stopped, and then continued. She tried to scream, but only a whimper came out. The gag in her mouth tasted of grease, and she fought to halt the bile tinged with a hint of lime that rose up into her throat. If she made it out of this, she didn't see any more key lime pie in her future. She didn't want to die trussed up like a turkey in the trunk of a car.

Joshua? She couldn't believe it. Someone else must have come in after them, someone who watched her leave the safety of Ruby's. Tears and panic clogged her sinuses. Rebecca dragged in as much air as she could around the cloth stuffed in her mouth.

*Calm down Rebecca. Panic will only make it worse.* She couldn't afford to waste breath or energy like this. She sniffed in to clear her nose as much as possible. One, two, three, four, five. She silently counted each breath in through her nose, then out around the cloth in her mouth to a count of five again.

The car stopped and the engine shut off. She expected it, but the slam of the door startled her anyway. *It's true what people say*, she thought. *When one of your senses is deprived, another one kicks into high gear to make up for it.* Footfalls rounded the back of the car, crunching over gravel. Rebecca pulled her head back. The trunk opened and let in a burst of light, penetrating her blindfold. She couldn't have been out for long if the sun still burned this hot in the sky.

She rocked her body back and forth, trying to evade the hands that reached in to lift her out. Her foot made contact with a satisfying thud when she kicked her leg out, the one thing her captor neglected to bind.

"Ouch, stop it, or I'll have to knock you out again."

Fresh tears leaked out. *Oh god, Joshua, what have you done?* A door squeaked on its hinges and a woman called out, startling Rebecca into ceasing her struggles. "The room is ready. This way." Rebecca couldn't place the voice, it didn't sound familiar at all.

"Well done, Twelve." Another voice, this time a man's.

*Twelve what?* Rebecca landed on a bed. She jerked when hands fumbled with the knots behind her back. Once free, Rebecca inched her arms around front, rubbing to ease the pain searing through stiff muscles.

"Hold her legs down," the woman ordered right before she pulled Rebecca's T-shirt over her head.

"Argh." Rebecca screamed behind the gag, her upper body gyrating wildly. A knee pressed into her chest as fingers fumbled at the waistband of her jeans. Tears streamed down her face, and her throat grew raw from the screams trapped inside. The woman never faltered. Once she removed Rebecca's clothes, the woman gripped Rebecca's arms and tied them again, dragged them up over her head, and secured the rope to something near the top of the bed.

"Get her legs." Hands groped for her flailing ankles, male hands.

Rebecca tried to draw her knees up and twist away, but he was too strong. Her legs parted, stretched wide, and anchored to the bottom corners of the bed.

Rebecca writhed and shimmied knowing it made no difference, but unwilling to give in.

"Is she ready?" She recognized the man's voice from outside the car. There must only be three of them. She flinched when the flat of his hand, oily with some kind of residue, pressed against her stomach. The gurgled screaming started up again.

"It'll go easier on you if you cooperate."

*Cooperate? Are you kidding?* Rebecca shifted her hips back and forth to evade his touch. "We're not going to hurt you. Calm down. We're just looking for something."

Rebecca wondered where the hell they thought a naked woman could be hiding something, and then strained to press her thighs together. The man's hands roamed over the entire front of her body, even her armpits. When he moved to her hips she struggled anew. She heard a rustling and felt a faint warmth between her legs, like the heat of the lamp when her doctor did a pap smear. Fingers pulled at her pubic hair.

*What the hell were they looking for?*

"Turn her over." Calloused fingers untied her feet so the three of them could flip her onto her stomach. For some reason Rebecca felt even more vulnerable in this position.

The hands continued, moving slowly up and down each leg and between her toes. He moved up her back and into the crease at the nape of her neck.

"Nothing," he said.

"What about her scalp?" the woman asked.

They untied Rebecca's wrists and pushed her up onto her spread knees. The woman gave her shoulders a shake. "Sit still." Rebecca felt the same heat, on her scalp this time. He moved each section of hair in an orderly fashion. The smell of peanut oil rose from his fingers.

"There!" he shouted out, pulling the hair away just behind and above her left ear.

*Oh goody, he found it, now maybe they'll leave me alone.*

"Let me see," the woman said. "It's different. Almost the same, but there's something else layered over it." Her fingers pinched Rebecca's chin, turning her. "Have you had any tattoos done on your scalp?"

Rebecca shook her head.

"I don't know what this means," the woman said. "Do you?"

Whoever she asked must have answered with a nod or shake of the head, or not at all. "We need to check with One before we can decide what to do with her. Make sure she's securely tied. You don't need me to remind you what will happen if she escapes," her voice faded with her departing footsteps.

Rebecca knew the heavy sigh came from Joshua. He laid her down on her back and retied her hands over her head. He left her legs together this time, leaving about six inches of loose rope between them. After anchoring the rope to something at the foot of the bed, he draped a thin sheet over her, covering her up to her chin. Rebecca turned her face away, refusing to show gratitude for the delayed concession to her modesty.

# Chapter Twenty-Two

Dan surveyed the parking lot for Rebecca's car. "Dammit." He smacked his hand on the steering wheel. "I know it took longer than I said, but she promised she'd stay here."

Finn turned to Dan. "It sounded more like you coerced her, but who am I to judge?" He ignored the look Dan sent his way. "Three weeks ago you couldn't keep your hands off each other. Now, it's a rare thing to find each of you on the same side of the room. I'm thinking the two of you had a parting of the ways. Then yesterday you just about bit my head off for greeting the lass with an innocent peck on the cheek, for God's sake. What gives? You two love birds have a spat?"

"Our relationship is not up for discussion," Dan bit out. "And Rebecca is very much still taken, so keep your mitts to yourself." Dan cringed inwardly at the desperate possession in his voice. "Getting Sabrina back is Rebecca's sole focus. Mine too."

Finn laughed. "You've got it bad mate." Dan rubbed the shoulder Finn's big mitt just connected with. "I'm insulted you'd think I'd poach on your property. It's against code, man." Finn's face turned serious. "Let's go in and see if anyone saw Rebecca leave."

Dan caught Ruby just inside the door with an armful of dirty dishes. "Have you seen Rebecca?"

"She left earlier." Ruby continued to the cart and unloaded the dishes.

"Did you see when? Did she leave alone?"

Ruby pulled her order pad from the pocket on her apron. "It's a madhouse in here today. The ghost town has some special event everyone's headed out to tonight, and they're all stopping here for a bite to eat first. It's a good problem to have, but I'm shorthanded. I haven't even had a chance to visit the ladies room."

A customer raised her arm. "Miss, can you take our order now? We don't want to be late."

"Be right there." She rolled her eyes at Dan. "I'm sorry, I can't offer more."

"Sure. I'll let you get back to work. Thanks." Dan headed out, but stopped beside the car. "I've got a bad feeling about this. Let's head back to the house, see if she's there." He tossed his cellphone in Finn's lap. "Her cell number's three on speed dial."

Finn tried her cellphone while Dan broke every speed limit on the way to Rebecca's house. "She's not answering. The house number two?" At Dan's nod, Finn dialed. "No answer there either."

"Shit."

"Could be she's just pissed at you and not picking up," Finn suggested, waving the phone at him. "I am using your phone after all."

"I hope you're right." Dan drove in silence the last few miles. He took the last corner on the edge of his wheels. "Her car's not in the driveway."

Both men headed for the front door at the same time. Finn put a hand on Dan's shoulder, stopping him a foot away. He had his gun in his hand and placed a finger to his lips. He gestured up. Dan looked up to see empty space where the thread Finn left on the top of the door once rested. When the door swung inward with the push of his finger, Dan pulled his gun from its harness. Giving Finn the signal to circle around back, Dan went in the front door low.

Nothing looked out of place. He lowered his gun hand to his side, and checked the living room. He saw Finn through the window in the back door shaking his head. Nothing. Dan did a quick sweep upstairs while Finn checked the main floor.

Dan bounded down the stairs at the squeal of tires in the distance, but no sign of the car appeared by the time he reached the back of the house. "Shit." Dan ran over to the tree line, good cover if a person went looking for it. Fresh tire tracks marked the trail.

"They must have hid the car and walked in." Finn caught up and bent down. "Hey now, what's this?" Dan walked over to get a better look at the letter lying in the dirt. "You think it might be another warning?"

"Or something." Dan didn't want to dwell on the *or something*.

Finn read the note over Dan's shoulder. "Time is running out. There's less time than you think." Finn leaned back against the car.

131

"Well, that's not good."

A crude map covered the bottom half of the page. No address, just a few intersecting streets, with a single letter labeling each. L, D, and H. A large X marked the bend of the street labeled H.

"Ryker will plug that into Bella, and she'll find it. There can't be that many intersecting roads around here with those initials and that configuration."

"The writing on this is different from the last warning. Let's head back to town. We'll ask around again, try to retrace her steps." Dan fumbled with the car keys, and then cursed when he dropped them. As he bent down to pick them up, he pointed to the tire tread in the dirt. "Finn?"

Finn came around and crouched next to Dan. "What have we here?" Finn met Dan's eyes. "That's the tread of a tire with a nail in it."

"Joshua's tire?"

"That'd be my guess."

Dan grabbed the keys from the dirt.

On the drive back to town, Finn suggested Rebecca may have taken her car to Josh. "Call the team and have them meet us at the garage. Joshua has an apartment above it." Dan headed straight to Joshua's garage and pulled up out front. They found a note taped to the door.

"Closed due to death in the family," Dan read. The note went on to list the contact info for one of Joshua's back-up mechanics. Dan pulled out the letter and held it up next to the note on the door. A perfect match.

"I thought Ryker said Bishop didn't have any family."

"That's what his report said. Both parents dead. No siblings. It didn't mention distant relatives." They headed around back to find the door locked, and a quick look through the window showed no sign of the Buick. The team's car rounded the corner and pulled to a stop next to Dan.

\* \* \* \*

Evan, Ryker, Nick, and Kaden stepped out of the Pathfinder. Evan opened the back hatch, lifted the floor panel, and unzipped the duffel bag hidden beneath it.

"Where's your car?"

"Out front." Dan placed his keys in Ryker's outstretched hand. His eyes followed Finn, Kaden, and Nick up the fire escape stairs to the apartment above. Kaden pulled a case from her pocket and went to work on the lock upstairs. Evan and Ryker did the same at the rear door to the garage. They made it inside in forty-five seconds.

Ryker opened the bay doors and moved both vehicles inside, while Evan and Dan made their way to the office area. They stopped short in the waiting room doorway. A string of expletives flew from Dan's lips at the sight of the magazines scattered over the floor. A take out container and a piece of pie lay on its side on a resin table right next to a full coffee cup and a green bag.

"I take it that's Rebecca's purse?" Evan deduced.

"I found Rebecca's car in the far bay." Ryker walked into the room. "Well, shit."

Evan opened the door at the end of the office area, revealing a set of stairs that presumably led to Joshua's apartment above. "Let's see what the others have found," he said and started up. Dan picked up Rebecca's purse and turned to Ryker. "I never should have left her alone."

"Let's get her back." Ryker grabbed hold of Dan's arm, nudging him toward the stairs leading to the small apartment above.

A green floral sofa that looked like a seventies reject stood behind a laminate coffee table covered with dishes, a few mugs, and several beer bottles. Finn and Evan rifled through drawers and cupboards in the small kitchen. Dan figured the rustling coming from the next room had to be Kaden.

"Got something."

They moved en-mass to the bedroom. Dan walked across the thin mattress lying on the floor and peered into the closet. "What is it?"

"Not sure yet," Kaden's muffled voice came from the back corner. She held a screwdriver wedged between her teeth while she worked at a panel with the blade of her Night Force. She sat back on her heels with a grunt of satisfaction a few seconds later. She placed the knife and screwdriver on the floor next to her, gently working the panel loose, and turned her head. "Looks like our friend Joshua has himself a little hidey-hole. I've almost got it." A smile spread across her face. "I'm in." She pulled out an old book and handed it to Dan.

The musty brown leather cover showed no title. He checked the spine and found it blank as well. Dan blew off a layer of dust and rubbed his fingers across the raised pattern centered on the cover.

"Does this mean anything to you?" Dan held the book out for Evan to see. Kaden put away her tools and stood up. "Let me take a look." Taking the book, she studied the pattern for a bit, flipping through the first few pages with care. "If this is what I think, we may have just found what this cult would consider their bible."

Ryker appeared in the bedroom doorway, Sig in hand. "We've got company. Cop at our door step." Kaden screwed the panel back in place and packed up her gear in seconds. Ryker waved them down the inside staircase into the office, tossing Dan his keys just as they heard the door to the apartment slam open. Evan came to a rolling stop long enough for Ryker to jump in the back seat, and then peeled off. Dan pulled out close behind in his SUV, Kaden sitting next to him. A bullet whizzed past Dan's bumper as he rounded the corner on two wheels and raced through the intersection.

"Why would a cop break into Bishop's apartment?" Evan flew past, continuing up Sloan Avenue.

Kaden holstered the Glock, her weapon of choice. "Maybe because he didn't have an official reason to be there?" She pulled out the book. The thin pages crackled as she turned them. "What I'm seeing here confirms the sacrifices are made on the child's birthday." She paused. "Of course, that explains it."

"Explains what?" Dan and the rest of the guys appreciated Kaden's speed reading skill, it came in handy, but often left the team playing catch-up.

"The eighteen month overlaps. Each child is born with a mark that looks like this." She held the book up.

Dan frowned. "A heptagon?"

"Right. The basic form. This mark identifies the chosen ones. It symbolizes feelings and instincts of a group, and containment. When they're four and a half years old this tattoo, an obtuse heptagram," she turned the page and held the book up again, "is applied over the existing mark, creating a new symbol. The tattoo must be applied eighteen months before sacrifice. That's why they have two girls at once."

Dan glanced over and saw the symbol sketched on the yellowed page. "Any idea what that signifies?"

"It goes back to the number seven. Several symbols apply to the various theories. This appears to be a combination of two of those symbols. On its own, the second image symbolizes passivity. Contentment is achieved by attuning with nature." She shrugged. "Combined with the first it could symbolize attuning with the group. Taking away the binds that contain the group mind in the first symbol opens the communication channels. This takes time to achieve, according to what's written here, which is why it's done eighteen months before the sacrifice." She turned the page. "A third symbol is applied a few days before the ceremony. An acute heptagram."

Dan glanced over at the seven-sided star. "That's an occult symbol isn't it? Used in witchcraft?"

"On its own, yes it's one of many used in witchcraft. It usually suggests heightened sensitivity, interaction, and progression. In this case, I believe it also represents the flow of energy between bodies."

"What does it mean when the three symbols are combined?"

"Combined, they'd represent a state of meditation. Perhaps the ultimate state." Kaden shook her head. "I have no idea how that fits into the final stages of the plan. Whatever it is, it has to happen on a certain day." She closed the book, but kept her place with her finger. "Finn said the warning left at Rebecca's suggested they've moved the time line up." She shook her head. "According to this book the flow of energy from one body to the next wouldn't happen, or would at the very least suffer, if the ceremony didn't happen on the ideal day."

"This isn't some fly-by-night organization. They've been around for decades, they'd know that. There has to be something to gain from doing it early."

"Or maybe we're getting too close and they have no choice. Do it a few days early, or wait another eighteen months."

"Maybe. If they're willing to chance it, they must be desperate. Desperate people don't care who gets hurt. They're only interested in the bottom line."

"Desperate people make mistakes Dan. That'll be their downfall." They rendezvoused with the rest of the team fifteen minutes later behind a deserted house on the outskirts of town.

# Chapter Twenty-Three

Rebecca rubbed her head against the mattress, maneuvering the blindfold until it shifted up enough for her to see out a thin crack at the bottom. The claustrophobia clawing at her crept back, allowing her to focus.

Rebecca experimented, tilting her head back to test how much she could see. She wouldn't be able to see their faces, not without doing a handstand, but could see the floor if she stood up. Enough to know where to place her feet when she ran.

Rebecca flinched when the door opened. Soft hands worked at the ties on her wrists. The woman again, she thought. As the knots loosened, something hard and cold poked Rebecca's stomach.

"Feel this?" she asked.

Rebecca nodded.

"It's a gun. I may not be allowed to kill you, but I won't hesitate to hurt you. Understood?"

Rebecca nodded again, recognizing the woman as the bigger threat of the pair of captors. She jerked when something soft landed on her stomach.

"I'm going to untie your hands. You are going to put your clothes on. Quickly. You can untie your feet to put your pants on. If your hands go near the blindfold at any time I will shoot you." The barrel of the gun pressed against the side of her knee. Once you're dressed I'll let you visit the bathroom. Then I'll be tying you up again so don't get any ideas." She untied the final knot.

Rebecca brought her hands down, her muscles screaming, and rubbed at her raw wrists. She fumbled with the clothes in her lap, identifying each piece by feel. She pulled the bra on, then the T-shirt. Pins and needles stabbed at her fingers as she worked at the knots by her ankles. After shimmying into her panties and jeans, she swung her legs over the side of the bed and waited. The woman's grip pinched her upper arm.

"On your feet. I haven't got all day." Again, the cold pressure of the gun barrel drilled in, this time at her ribs. The woman waited there while Rebecca used the toilet and washed her hands. Rebecca splashed water on her face, and then turned to where she thought the woman stood and mimed drinking from a glass.

"Don't make a sound." She pressed a glass into Rebecca's hands and tugged the gag out of her mouth. Rebecca reached out with her free hand until her she connected with the faucet and filled the glass. The cold water soothed her throat, parched from hours of breathing around a gag. She refilled it and chugged once more before the woman grabbed the glass from her.

"That's enough. I don't want to have to go through this nonsense too often." She replaced the gag and shoved Rebecca forward again. They must be planning to keep her here for a while. Good, that gave her more time to plan her escape.

God, the heat drained her. No air conditioning or fan in the bedroom, and the closed window only made it worse. Rebecca's steps slowed on the way back to the room. She understood the primal instinct of animals better now. Lying on her back, vulnerable, held no appeal. When they got back to the room Rebecca sat on the bed and scootched until her back hit the wall. She held out her hands, and hoped the woman would take the hint to tie her up in a sitting position.

"Suit yourself." Rebecca heard the sneer in her voice. "You'll still be tied up." The rough rope circled Rebecca's wrists again. She left Rebecca's hands in front before wrapping the rope around her waist twice and anchoring it to the bed frame again.

Rebecca wouldn't be able to lie down or move much at all, but she preferred it over a position of weakness. A sigh escaped Rebecca when the woman left, leaving her legs unbound. Something pink lay on the mattress. She reached down with her fingers and snagged the small square of paper; the gum wrapper she fiddled with earlier today. She must have stuck it in her pocket when she got back to the parking lot.

Rebecca leaned her head back against the headboard, crossed her legs, and let her hands rest in her lap. Never once did Joshua cross her mind as a suspect. How many other friends and acquaintances grieved alongside of her, all the while knowing Bree's whereabouts? Her own husband betrayed her and she'd been clueless.

Rebecca shook her head. *Stop this.* She needed to find a way out of there, not wallow in self-pity. The mattress, bare but for the dingy sheet covering Rebecca, took up the center of the room. She tilted her head back as far as possible and spied a high window to the left of the bed. Faint light filtered through hideous chartreuse curtains, allowing Rebecca to see daylight fading fast. Dan and his team would likely move under the cover of darkness, and she held onto that hope as she continued her survey of the room.

On her right, the door to the room stood slightly ajar. Other than the bed, the room was empty of anything she could use as a weapon. The light barely penetrated the gap in the bottom of the blindfold now, no matter how far back she craned her neck. Warped walls were held together by several layers of peeling wallpaper that misguided souls must have put up in numerous desperate attempts to disguise the bleak, dreary room. Dark water streaks trailed over the paper from ceiling to floor. It hit her then.

The room from her visions—Bree on this very bed, crying for her mother and waiting to be rescued. Terrified and confused. Rebecca moved to bring her hands to her face but stopped when the rope tied around her waist tightened. Dammit. She stretched her fingers down instead. Maybe making contact with her bare skin on the mattress would bring on a vision. She blanked her mind of all thoughts but Bree, visualizing bright lights protruding out, like reaching fingers. *Feel me, baby. Reach out to me. I'm coming for you.* Nothing.

Rebecca flicked the gum wrapper across the room in disgust. *Stupid, stupid girl.* Visions couldn't be forced, she *knew* that. If lying naked on the bed for hours hadn't stimulated a vision, what made her think touching the mattress with her fingertips would do it?

*Dan, where are you?* He'd have questioned people at Ruby's by now. A dozen or more people filled the place. Someone must have seen her talking to Joshua, leaving with him. Who? Think dammit. Norman Parks sat in the corner booth reading the paper, coughing and sputtering. But had he seen her?

Dan would be frantic by now. He already felt responsible for Bree; she'd made sure of it. Now he'll blame himself for her abduction, even though she wouldn't be in this mess if she did what he said. Surely he remembered her plan to speak to Josh, and about looking at her car.

Her anger at Dan was little more than camouflage for her disappointment in herself. In the end, Dan uncovered Pete's secrets.

Honestly, Dan attracted her from the beginning, back during the initial investigation. But recognizing it and acting on it were two different things, and she'd been in no condition to do either. Devastation and rage masked her feelings at first. Later, much later, the attraction resurfaced, but guilt over putting herself before Bree made her push Dan away. She became downright nasty to him the days before he moved the CARD team back to the field office. She all but shoved him out the door, for God's sake, unable to face her guilt. To his credit, he took most of it with gentle smiles and compassion, until that last day. He made the decision to leave days before, she realized now, because he knew she *needed* him to. Not because he gave up on finding Bree, or because they gave into a mutual desire for escape, however brief. Rebecca rested her head against the wall and prayed she'd get to see him one more time if only to apologize. And maybe tell him she loved him.

The front door of the house slammed shut, jarring Rebecca from her memories. Angry voices carried down the hall, too muffled for her to make out, at first, until they got closer.

"One wants her brought in tonight. He's moving things up again." A man, Rebecca guessed.

"I can't believe he'd do that."

The fear in the woman's voice intrigued Rebecca.

"Are you questioning One's leadership?"

A ticked off man, Rebecca concluded.

"Of course not."

"So it's me you doubt." The newcomer's voice poked at her memory.

"There's always a danger when plans change and we're forced to improvise. That's when mistakes happen."

"Bring her in tonight, when your shift ends."

"What did One say about the mark?" The Nut asked. He ate so many peanuts he reeked of them. Peanuts in the shell. Even from here, she heard the crackle as he broke through the outer layer, and the crunch as he walked across them on the floor. Dubbing him The Nut seemed to fit. That, and the fact that he was crazy. They all were.

"He seemed pleased. He mentioned something about doubling the power source but we were interrupted, and he never finished his thought. I'm not sure how it affects the ceremony other than moving it forward once again." His voice grew louder, closer. "I want to see it."

The door opened. Someone shone a bright light on Rebecca's head while The Nut fiddled with her hair.

"Remarkable." Rebecca smelled sweetened stale coffee on the stranger's breath. Damn, she knew that voice. Where had she heard it? Of course, the man who'd been talking to Chief Bains on the other side of the ER curtain. A shiver of revulsion rippled through her when he stroked a finger along her cheek. The revulsion receded, replaced by a stab of pain at her temple.

Bree. An image flashed in her head, with Bree's signature. The bastard must have touched her baby recently. Skin to skin contact triggered a vision once before, when the officer who came to tell her father about her mother's fatal car accident reached over and brushed Rebecca's hair behind her ear. An image of her mother flared before her, bloody and pale, hunched over the steering wheel of a burning car. Rebecca had buried her face in her father's neck and started sobbing. When the officer left, she lifted her head. "Mommy's never coming home," she whispered, and watched the look of shock on her father's face turn to dread. Fortunately, grief, and the chaos of the next few days distracted him. He never spoke to her about that night again. That night she lost her mother and gained her visions.

"Give it a couple more hours, then it should be plenty dark enough," the stranger said. "You'll need to be careful. A bloody freak show is on at the ghost town tonight. Damn place is swarming with tourists all hyped up. Convinced they'll see Indian spirits protecting the mines, and if they're lucky, the vengeful ghosts of the murdered miners too. I'm supposed to be there now handling crowd control. I don't understand why people believe this shit. If you ask me, it's all a myth created to drive revenue to the state. Ghosts don't exist."

Their laughter faded as they moved out of the room. The woman and her flunky left Rebecca alone for the next hour or so, she couldn't tell for sure how much time passed in the dark. Rebecca spent the time resting, conserving her energy. Escape held no interest for her now. Before long, they'd be on their way to see the man in charge. She'd lay odds the leader stayed close to the children. Why escape someone about to take her exactly where she wanted to be?

* * * *

Kaden filled in the team on the details in the book while Dan worked with Ryker on the map. They must be holding her close by. Close enough to town to get to the meeting spot and back on foot most of the way, in an evening. Joshua put in an appearance every day since Dan moved into Rebecca's. He most likely traveled at night. Near enough for him to get at least a couple hours of sleep so he could get through the next day at work. A guy can only pull so many all-nighters.

Ryker took a picture of the map and sent it to Bella who ran some kick ass program that overlaid the image on a map of local streets. Despite Finn's prediction, Bella came up with four possible areas. They discarded the two on the west side of Phoenix and concentrated on the remaining two, one here in town, the other out by the Peaks.

"Why don't we split up?" Dan folded the map and put it back in his pocket.

Evan shook his head. "We have to consider this is a set-up."

"Of course, and we can't go to Chief Bains." Finn strapped on his webbing and checked his gear. "He's got at least one dirty cop in his house. What other lead do we have?"

"We're wasting time here."

Nick slapped Dan on the back. "Being careful is never a waste of time. Let's take the house in town first. It's on the way to the Peaks anyway."

Dan's cellphone rang while they geared up, and Nick read the display over Dan's shoulder.

"Bains?" Nick asked.

Dan nodded, and took a few steps away from the noise of the team to answer the call. "Thanks Chief, I appreciate the head's up." He hung up and walked back to where the others waited, geared up, and ready to go.

142

"They've found the Reynolds', dead and dumped outside of Tucson. The chief took the call this afternoon."

Finn holstered his Sig. "No sign of the kid?"

Dan shook his head. "He wanted me to know about a piece of paper found lodged in the throat of Mrs. Reynolds. It said 'Grace knows.' They couldn't make out the rest of it, but the next word started with 'wh.' The Tucson police remembered the report Bains sent them on Jennifer Reynolds last month and decided to keep him in the loop."

"Grace knows. Grace is the neighbor right?"

Dan nodded. "I got the impression she could give us more, but I have no idea what she knows."

"Keep thinking on it as we go," Evan said. "Let's move 'em out."

Fifteen minutes later, they drove into an older community on the edge of town. Down on their luck houses, widely spaced, dotted the street. Only three on the bend the X had pinpointed. They parked a block away and doubled back. Evan signaled for Kaden and Nick to take the first house they came to. The well-lit house had several cars in the driveway. Evan and Ryker took the second house, while Dan and Finn continued, stopping at the one on the bend of the road.

The house sat in darkness, whisper quiet, with no car in the drive. Dan kept his gun hand by his side as he rounded the corner, checking windows and curtains as he went. Finn jimmied a lock and lifted himself up and over the ledge. Dan went in behind him. The search ended almost before it began. With two bedrooms, a bathroom and a single room at the front, the house redefined small. They found empty cupboards and a lot of dust, but not much else. It didn't look like anyone lived there until recently. They found half a carton of fresh milk in the fridge, and an ashtray on the table filled with lipstick stained Camel cigarette butts.

Dan checked the bathroom next. Dirt and stale cigarette smoke filled this room too. The medicine cabinet door hung on busted hinges. Dan nudged it open to find an empty pill bottle and a box of tampons. The patient and doctor names were ripped off, but enough of the label remained to identify Lorazepam as the contents. Serious knock out drugs.

Dan found Finn in the bedroom crouching by the head of the bed. "They restrained someone here." Finn pointed to a length of rope about nine inches long caught on the metal bed frame, some of the strands stained red. With blood? He didn't want to linger on that image. "What's this?" Finn reached over and picked up a small square of pink paper. He unfolded it. "Bubble gum? You think they kept the kids here?"

"Shit. Let me see that." Dan kicked the foot of the bed. "Dammit. We missed her."

The rest of the team joined them. "Third one's the charm, I see."

"This is the house." Dan held up the wrapper. "This is Rebecca's. I saw her folding this in the parking lot earlier today."

"They've moved her then." Kaden's hand patted Dan's shoulder. "We just need to figure out where. Any more thoughts on the 'Grace knows' clue?"

Dan paced the floor. "Grace knew they left town quickly, that they drove, that they moved there from here." He held his hands to his temples. "Think dammit. She mentioned John feeling out of shape, that he missed hiking the local trails."

"Which trails?" Ryker prompted.

Dan's eyes flew to Ryker. "Red Eye. That's where we found Jennifer Reynold's body. Shit, who buries a body right next to the scene?"

"Criminals are stupid, you know that. Let's head back to the car and I'll have Bella search for abandoned caves in that area."

"The Peaks are full of abandoned caves Ryker, remember the gold mines?" Kaden asked.

"Yes, but back in the sixties they closed a lot of the tunnels to tourists after noticing instability and danger of collapse. My guess is this group has found themselves a condemned section of tunnels to set up shop in."

Using the bed as his desk Ryker put Bella to work, focusing on the Red Eye caves. "Bingo." Dan leaned his head in the window to get a look. "Red Eye has a condemned section over here, never opened to the public, due to cave-ins during the twenties. In fact, the town redesigned the landscape to direct people away from that section. It looks like most tourists bought the misdirection." He hit a few more keys. "No reports of any teenagers breaking in for late night parties, and no eager tourists looking for lost gold in this particular spot, just the occasional rock climber. This could be it."

"Did you see that?"

Finn looked at Dan. "See what, Mate?"

"The blinking red light."

* * * *

Two stood in the shadows watching them enter his trap, one by one. A smile spread across his face when the last of them disappeared through the open window. *These guys keep butting their noses into places they have no right to be. Someone needs to teach them a lesson. If they're too stupid to survive it, so be it.* He slipped the disposable cellphone out of his pocket, dialed the number he'd committed to memory and hit send.

The ground beneath his feet trembled as the explosion lit up the night sky.

# Chapter Twenty-Four

Joshua and the woman with him received the honor of dressing Rebecca for the ceremony. When they removed the blindfold at the entrance to the caves, Rebecca focused on the opportunity to keep an eye out for Bree and pushed the thought of what the action implied to the back of her mind. She watched Josh rummage through a tote bag on the floor in the corner and didn't notice the woman approach until she grabbed her arm and jabbed a needle in. Rebecca jerked away, knocking it to the floor and grinding it under her foot. Swinging her bound hands up, she aimed for the woman's face, grunting at the satisfying crunch of fist connecting with nose.

"You bitch."

A smile tugged at the corner of Rebecca's mouth when she saw blood dribble down the woman's chin.

Before she could celebrate her tiny victory, the room swayed under her feet, and Rebecca fell to the floor. On the drive here, she overheard the woman and The Nut mention a drug they used to paralyze their captives. A drug that paralyzed without numbing. They liked their victims aware, terrified, and helpless during the ceremony. Apparently, adrenalin infused blood provided an extra kick. Bastards. Once immobilized, Rebecca couldn't cause trouble during the big event. She fought off the paralytic effects and prayed that she knocked the syringe to the ground before the full dose went in.

Joshua walked toward her, a ball of white fabric in his hands. He and the woman worked in silence while they replaced her clothing with a full-length white gown, suitable for a sacrifice she supposed. She learned a lot on the drive over here tonight.

"Is she ready?" The voice of the man she heard talking to Bains at the hospital grew louder as he approached. "For god's sake be careful. One won't be happy if you get blood on her. Clean yourself up before he sees you."

The woman's feet moved toward the opening, and then disappeared from Rebecca's line of sight. The connection between brain and muscle no longer functioned. Grains of dirt scratched at her cheek on the cave floor, surprisingly cool against skin flushed from her futile attempts to command her body to move.

The man jerked her arm, rolling her from her side to her back. Fire shot through the shoulder he wrenched on.

"Help me lift her onto the cart." Two sets of hands grabbed her arms and legs and swung her up, knocking her head on something sharp as they pulled her up, before dropping her with a thump on a hard surface. Damn, that confirmed it, she could still feel pain.

"Grab that bag and bring it, will you?" The man said to Joshua. Rebecca heard a loud thunk, followed by a thud. The sound of pounding, accompanied by grunts and moans went on for several seconds, ending with a sickening crunch. Footsteps edged closer.

*Please be Joshua. Please be Joshua.*

"Time to go." The grinning face looming over her didn't belong to Joshua, but Rebecca recognized it nonetheless. Officer Turner. A scream rose up, only to remain trapped in her throat.

# Chapter Twenty-Five

Emily and Tricia hovered over Bree as she lay on the cave floor. Bree sensed their panic, and squeezed Emily's hand in encouragement. Emily rewarded her with a tiny smile, while Tricia hid her face in Bree's lap. Bree warned them this might happen. Ever since Carrie taunted her with the pain her mother felt when a forced vision hit her, Bree tried experimenting with ways to reverse the effect. Surrounded by the waves of power within the caves, the strength of her own abilities increased as did Emily's and Tricia's. When Emily suggested they practice and bravely offered herself up as guinea pig, Bree took her up on it.

The opportunity to practice came sooner than expected. The sour faced man gave them the same pills as always, Bree could tell from the bottle, but they didn't work the way they did back at the house. None of them fell asleep after taking them anymore. The guards still made jokes about not letting the bed bugs bite, so Bree didn't think they knew something had changed. She told the girls not to let on about the drugs, to act like everything remained the same. This gave them control, something they needed more of. Once the guards gave them their nighttime pills, they didn't return until morning. That gave them lots of practice time.

But the time for testing ended. Either it worked or it didn't. Bree concentrated on sending the message to Dan, visualized a path of light leaving her and traveling through the caves. In the past, she could only sense Dan in her room, but lately, their connection grew stronger. She felt him now, still too far away, but nearer than before.

Bree cried out when the light flickered, but forced it back into focus. She still needed to get the tricky part of her plan to work. She had to get the message to Dan, but hold back the pain that flowed with it. Bree didn't know much about bombs, except what she saw in the odd TV show they let her watch at the house. She sent the image of a blinking red light, the easiest symbol she could think of, and hoped Dan knew what it meant.

The blowback of the vision brought instant tears. Emily's gasp echoed Bree's, and Bree's grip on her hand tightened just before blackness engulfed her.

* * * *

Dan followed the others, diving into the dry gulley running along the back of the house as the blast exploded around them.

They crawled along the ditch for twenty minutes before stopping.

Finn took a swig of water while Kaden tended to the wound on his arm. "Christ, I don't want to be cutting it that close again."

Ryker laughed. "Guess there's no longer any question of a trap."

Kaden put the med kit away. "I can't wait to see their faces when they realize we're not that easy to kill."

Dan rose, extended a hand to Finn. "Let's move out."

"I'm still not clear on what you saw, mate," Finn paused long enough to get Dan to look back at him, "and I'm not gonna ask you to explain. I owe you. Big time. That's all I need to know."

Dan walked backwards. "Finding the girls and taking these bastards down marks all debts paid in full."

Finding several cars in the Red Eye pay station lot erased any doubts they had the right place. Dan led the team in to the spot where they discovered Jennifer Reynolds' remains, and then turned the lead over to Ryker. The difficult trail became treacherous in the dark. The township did a damn good job disguising it. No one would naturally gravitate to a path leading away from the peak. Before long, the team took a turn, almost doubling back until they came to a wall that seemed to support the aggressive plant life leaning against it. The dry creek running off the peak fed the local vegetation, creating an oasis of sorts in the immediate area during the winter months.

Finn reached over and shifted a section of hedge. A dark hole gaped behind it.

Dan turned off his flashlight and put on his night vision goggles. "We enter here. If they're advancing the schedule and doing the ceremony tonight, chances are the kids are here as well."

"Ryker and I will see to finding and securing the children." Evan checked his weapon. "Dan, you and Finn go after Rebecca. Kaden and

Nick, handle anyone who gets in our way."

"With pleasure." Kaden shifted the hedge and moved inside, the other's following close behind.

They heard the chanting first, growing louder as they traveled further into the cave. Dan increased his pace as the intensity built. Torches on the wall lit the way as they rounded the final bend. Dan's heart stopped. He removed his night vision goggles and saw Rebecca, covered in blood, prone on some kind of altar and a man standing over her wielding a dagger.

# Chapter Twenty-Six

Trickles of blood trailed over Rebecca as she lay on the smooth stone. She had no idea which section of the Peaks they brought her to. Certainly not one set up for public tours. That much she could tell.

The flowing gown dragged on the ground while two people carried her out and placed her on a natural shelf jutting out from the wall. Rebecca laid there for what seemed like hours. Hooded figures moved about, preparing for her death, but otherwise ignored her until a few moments ago. Now Norman Parks, the sadistic bastard, stood over her dribbling blood from some golden cup. Why didn't she realize his penchant for perfectly poached eggs hid a deeper flaw? He led a chant with the others, in a language she didn't understand.

The chamber, at least sixteen by twenty feet, seemed large compared to some of the mining tunnels in the area, but felt crowded with so many people. Unlike the tunnels open to the public, these walls appeared to be crumbling. Small rocks and dust cascaded down at the slightest provocation. A film of dust coated Rebecca where she lay mostly paralyzed, mixing with the blood Parks dribbled over her to create a pulpy paste. She hadn't seen Sabrina yet, but heard one of the hooded figures giving orders for another to get the children.

God, she sensed her presence.

Three openings led off the chamber, one remained dark, apparently unused by the group, while torches anchored into the walls at the entrances lit the other two. Rebecca could see both entrances from her prone position. One led to where Josh took her to get changed. There must be more than one room off that line, because the cloaked figure disappeared down that same off-shoot when instructed to get the child. That's the one, Rebecca decided. She'd head for that tunnel. As soon as she could move.

She tested her wrists again, managing to shift them slightly in their crossed position over her chest. The heaviness of the drug was wearing off from the top down. Her head could move, but until now, anything below her neck remained stubbornly frozen. She cursed the drugs clouding her system and closed her eyes at the thought of any child suffering through this. Their fear and panic would be overwhelming. She tested her legs, and her toes wiggled. A little more time, and her legs would hold her weight.

Their use of a generic numbering system in place of names suggested an organized, if not creative, group. Each had their role, from delivering the chalice to their apparent leader, Parks, to placing wrapped mystery bundles around the edges of the fire. Certain members stepped forward at times, playing solo roles in the chant while scattering a powder of some sort over the flames. The rest, mere observers, appeared content to form a sort of back-up choir. Aside from Parks, and the officer from the hospital, Rebecca didn't recognize any of the others. Going on height alone, one or two could be Pete, but neither would even look in her direction. Cowards, hiding behind their cloaks, thinking they're invisible to justice or consequence.

Parks faced away from her now, pouring some of the blood in the goblet over the flames as the group chanted. Barely a foot of space separated them, not enough for Rebecca to jump down and run, even if she could. A jagged edged dagger lay on the pulpit next to him, close enough for her to notice the intricate carvings in the ivory handle.

The chants rose in volume and intensity, sending shivers down Rebecca's spine. An eerie moan wrapped around the chamber, like the sleepy protest of a slumbering animal whose rest was interrupted. She appeared to be the only sacrifice here, so the moaning had to be echoes of the chanting. What else could it be? Her vision continued to clear as the drug wore off. Whatever they planned must be happening soon. She wiggled her ankles trying to swing her legs over the side and ended up crossing her ankles.

Parks turned to face her again. Shit. He dipped his finger into the gold goblet reaching over her to draw a pattern, sort of like a pentagram, but not, on the wall. He dipped his finger in again, this time tracing it over his face. War paint. Panic, all too real and expected under the circumstances, coursed through her, carrying sensation to dormant limbs. Her upper body inched away in revulsion. Parks, too far gone to notice or care, continued with the ritual. His face bore a natural flush, heightened by the heat of the fire and smears of blood. Spittle flew from his mouth when he coughed, scattering red dots over her white gown. *Dear god, did he drink the stuff?* Rebecca closed her eyes on a shiver, opening them again when his red tipped fingers trailed across her cheeks.

The chanting resumed. Flames shot up, carrying large shadows to the ceiling. Rebecca blinked and watched an Indian headdress outline crawl up the wall to the ceiling. Everyone in this room, except her, wore hoods. None wore an Apache ceremonial headdress. Time to ponder this new mystery ran out when Parks reached over and picked up the knife. Tears carved tracks through the blood and dust on her face, mapping her end. The hiss of flames intensified as Parks raised the dagger over his head.

# Chapter Twenty-Seven

"No!" Dan's shout brought momentary silence.

Kaden and Nick went in, taking out the three people closest to them before Dan even made it into the chamber. Several heads turned, grunting in surprise when Dan pushed his way through them. Arms bounced off him, unable to contain his fury. Evan and Ryker spread out, keeping the hooded figures in their sights, while Finn held back, setting up to take out the man now holding the dagger to Rebecca's throat.

Dan saw Finn shake his head out of the corner of his eye. He couldn't get the shot without risking Rebecca.

Dan raised his gun. "Lower the knife, Parks." The old man didn't move. "Lower the fucking knife and step away from her."

A grin crept over the bastard's face. "I don't think so."

Dan's gun hand shook when a red line appeared on Rebecca's throat.

"Lower your gun or she dies here and now." He pulled Rebecca up to stand in front of him as the team rushed in. Now he backed Rebecca toward the unlit opening in the wall. They stumbled into the darkness.

Rebecca's cries drowned out Dan's curses. "Find Sabrina."

With the clan down, unconscious for the most part, Nick and Kaden followed the tunnel the others took in search of the children. Only one member stood and he pointed a gun at Finn. His hood fell back revealing the cop who chased them out of Joshua's place, Officer Turner.

"I've got this." Finn's Irish eyes weren't smiling now. "Go after her."

* * * *

With a nod, Dan grabbed a torch from the wall and tore down the tunnel after Rebecca, his hope for speed severely hampered by intense darkness. Light from the torch barely penetrated two feet in front of him.

Debris littered the upward slope, slowing Dan even more. Parks had a good head start, and knowledge of the layout, while Dan had to assess each opening and determine which one he took. He covered his head with his arms when the scattering of stones pelted him from above for several seconds. A moan, much like the one the team heard earlier, carried on the breeze that circled above him, closing in on his head.

A mumbled curse down the tunnel to his right made him take the turn at a run. The darkness lifted slightly, allowing Dan to spot an opening at the end of the tunnel. He sent up a silent thank you for the large moon hanging heavy and full in the night sky. What he assumed was just rubble underfoot ended up being a set of rotted wooden rails used to ferry bins of dirt out when the tunnels had first been dug.

The tunnel split in two, going another fifty feet or so in both directions before exiting the peak. Dan debated which route to take when he saw the silhouette of an Indian chief in the night sky through the tunnel on his left. He blinked and the image disappeared. *What the hell?* With no sane reason why, he followed the clue and his gut, and went left.

About ten feet from the opening, Rebecca reappeared, once again an unwilling shield for Parks. Dan took a few steps, enough to see the two-hundred foot drop-off behind them. The heels of Parks' boots flirted with fate on the edge of nothing.

"Not another inch or I toss her over."

Dan held his breath, afraid the slightest breeze might send Rebecca to her death. Rebecca's tortured eyes begged him as she said, "Please, go find Sabrina." She swayed and her knees buckled.

*What the hell had they done to her?* Dan made a move to grab her limp form but Parks shifted his arm to her waist. Refusing to give up his shield, he used his body to support her weight, his feet shifting a precious inch back in the process.

A current of air, barely a whisper at first, circled them. Dan watched in horror as it built in strength, buffeting the pair. Parks wobbled under the force, before regaining his footing, placing the dagger against Rebecca's throat once more. As suddenly as the wind came, it drifted away, stirring up dirt twenty feet further along the face of the peak. The cries of children drew Dan's eye for a split second, long enough for him to see Evan and Ryker peering out of the tunnel's mouth next to them.

"Sabrina?" Rebecca looked over, craning her neck to catch sight of her baby.

"Mommy." Dan saw a small face peek out before strong arms pulled her back to safety.

"We've got her Rebecca. She's okay. She's safe." Evan's voice carried over on the wind that returned to torment them.

"Please let me go to my daughter." Rebecca sobbed.

"You should have backed off. We gave you plenty of warnings, and yet you ignored every one of them. You just had to accept Sabrina's death and move on. Instead you made it harder on yourself, yearning for the one thing you can never have."

"But I can have her, she's right there."

"Too late, Rebecca. She has to die. Tonight. And so do you if we are to achieve ascension."

"It's over, Parks. Let her go." Dan raised the tip of his gun level with Parks' forehead. "Your only way out of here is through me. Sabrina's already out of your reach."

Another crease of blood formed where the knife-edge sank into Rebecca's neck. "Only the blood of the chosen can release me."

"Release you from what?" Dan shouted as the wind spun in fury around their feet.

"The prison of his decaying body." Everyone turned toward the man braced against the opening of the cave. Rebecca gasped at the sight of him. If not for his voice, she wouldn't have recognized the pulpy mass of flesh as Joshua's face. He cradled his mangled arm against his chest, his breath whistling through the gaping hole where his nose should have been. Blood sprayed out on a cough that just about brought him to his knees.

"You need to ascend before your diseased body gives out." An obscene laugh choked out of Joshua. "Surprised to see me? You need to find a better henchman. Turner doesn't know enough to make sure the job is done before heading back to play with his friends."

Parks swallowed. "Exactly, Joshua, I am dying. Ascending tonight will kill the cancer eating at me. I deserve this. Have I not been a good leader over the years?"

"Not really, no. You're clueless a lot of the time. I knew you held a meeting without me. I watched the entire thing. And aren't you wondering why the kids are still awake, I switched the drugs at the house when Carrie called me out there."

Parks shifted his gaze to the opening along the wall where the children still huddled, reluctant witnesses to the horror playing out before them. "I made the tough decisions." He jabbed a finger against his chest. "Me. No one else had the stomach for it. We all have worked towards this for decades. The entire collective will benefit with the ascension, you know that. Joshua, get Cooper's gun. Prove your allegiance and all will be forgiven."

"I don't think so, old man." Josh turned to Rebecca. "I'm sorry." His scream of rage rent the air as he pushed off the wall and headed straight for the pair balanced on the precipice. Parks threw Rebecca to the ground, and used both hands to fight off his newest assailant. Joshua shoved Rebecca away from the edge with his feet, while pushing at Parks. Dan could see the burst of adrenaline that carried him this far begin to fade. With one final shove, Joshua forced Parks to step back, onto nothing. Shock washed over his face as his arms wind milled. At the last minute, Parks reached for Joshua's shirt, pulling him to the edge.

"No!" Dan saw Rebecca stretch her hand out toward Joshua, who grabbed hold with panic in his eyes as he went over. Dan leaped, but not fast enough. A cry of horror screamed past his lips, joined by those in the tunnel next to him, when Rebecca rolled over the edge after Joshua.

Grateful for his night vision goggles, he scrambled forward on his stomach, afraid to look down. About eight feet below, on a narrow ledge, Rebecca lay motionless on her right side. Alone.

"Hold on babe. Just hold on a few minutes more and we'll get you off there." Ryker showed up, three little girls in tow. "Where's Evan?"

"I sent him back to the room where they kept us tied up. There's lots of rope there," Sabrina volunteered. She placed the hand of the youngest girl in the hand of the middle child and shooed them back to safety and out of the way. Dan almost smiled. As the oldest child there, she took her role as caregiver quite seriously. As Evan came running, she turned back to Dan. "My mother needs you now." Her sad eyes drifted toward the cliff edge. Ryker placed a gentle hand on her shoulder when she started toward it. "Hurry. She's running out of time."

Dan rushed to the edge, and sure enough, Rebecca stirred, shifting dangerously close to empty air. His eyes followed the crack near where the ledge met the wall. A small cloud of white dust swirled in the wind. The ledge crumbled before his eyes. The wind picked up again, whipping around them in fury. "Stay still," he shouted down to Rebecca, unsure if she heard him until he saw her left arm wave weakly. "Don't move an inch babe." He looked over his shoulder at Evan, now joined by Finn, Nick and Kaden. They worked furiously, tying lengths of rope together, creating a harness.

Dan looked down at Rebecca again. She'd have to get the harness over her head and under her armpits. Blood pooled where her head lay. Then he noticed her closed eyes and limp hand that only a moment before waved at him. "Shit." He looked at the team. "She's out cold. I'll need to put the harness on for her."

"There's no way that ledge can take your weight." Evan placed a restraining hand on Dan's shoulder.

"Let me go down." Sabrina stepped forward. "I don't weigh much at all. Tie me to one end of the rope and I can put the harness on her."

Kaden knelt down and took Sabrina in her arms. "That's very brave of you to offer sweetie, but we can't let you do that."

"She makes a good point," Finn said, rolling his eyes when they all looked at him like he'd gone insane. "I'm not thinking of sending the child down, for God's sake." He looked at Dan and grinned. "Just you. We can lower you down to Rebecca like the lass here said. You can get the harness on her without putting any weight on the ledge. No sweat. We've got this man."

Dan looked around, but found no place to anchor the rope on the dry, sandy ledge. "Without an anchor you can't hold both of us. Not even the five of you."

"There are anchors in the wall." Five pairs of eyes looked at Sabrina. "People sometimes climb this face," she frowned, "but not very often."

"They come and move us to another part of the tunnel, or they give us medicine that makes us go numb all over so we can't move or call for help." This came from the middle girl, Emily, who pointed at the spot where Rebecca had gone over. "They gave her some earlier, that's why she's just laying there." Dan's frustrated eyes met Finn's over her head.

"If the rope is long enough you can tie it to the tracks. Would they work as an anchor? They're pretty strong right here."

Kaden followed Sabrina back into the tunnel a few paces and tested the tracks where Sabrina stopped. She smiled and ruffled Sabina's amber curls.

"It's perfect," she said, loud enough for the others to hear. The team spent precious seconds rigging the rope before calling Dan over from his perch on the edge.

"When you get there put the harness on Rebecca and we'll pull you both up together. Hey!" Evan got Dan's attention. "You're planning some dumb ass move. I can see it in your eyes." He turned, throwing the harness to Nick. "Change in plans. You're going down instead."

"No!" Both Sabrina and Dan shouted together over the wind whipping around them.

"I'm going."

"It has to be him." She pointed to Dan. The wind whipped again, sending miniature dust funnels dancing across the ledge they stood on. Sabrina walked over to Dan and placed her palms against his cheeks when he knelt beside her. "Mommy needs you to get her." A gust of wind sent her curls flying. "Now!"

Dan looked over the edge again. The crack had lengthened, disappearing under Rebecca's still body. "I'm going." Dan stepped into the harness. Finn gave a firm tug on the rope, and secured the knot in back, while Ryker checked the front.

Evan tossed more rope to Kaden, who looped it around the tracks until it she got it firmly anchored. She straddled the rope, bracing her feet against one of the sturdier cross treads just inside the mouth of the cave. "Ready." She gave a tug on the rope. The others grabbed on.

Dan lowered himself over the side, bracing his feet on the wall. The rappel down went quick and uneventful. Hovering just above her, he gave the sign to the team and pushed out hard with his legs. They gave him just enough rope to bring him back in below the ledge. He came in, head level with Rebecca's. He brushed a finger over her cheek, afraid any more would set off a disastrous chain of events. "Hey there babe."

Rebecca smiled but didn't open her eyes. "Hey yourself. You're interrupting my nap."

He smiled back. "Tough. It's time to get up." She slid toward him a bit as the ledge tilted forward on a heavy groan. "The sooner the better." He lifted the harness over her head when he heard another groan, then a large crack. He grabbed her arms and wrapped them around his neck as he swung her legs around his waist.

"Now!" He wrapped his arms around her, looping his fingers through the rope circling her waist and pushed off hard just as the ledge dropped. When his feet reconnected with the wall, he pulled her close again. "Hang on," he whispered when her legs loosened around his hips and her head lolled on his shoulder. "If you can just hold on a few seconds more I'll take you up to see Sabrina." He spotted one of the clamps left behind by a climber and grabbed onto it with his left hand.

"Bree?"

"Yes, she's right there babe, waiting for you. Just hold on."

"I'm here mommy, do what he says for once, and hold on."

When Rebecca's arms tightened and her ankles crossed behind him, Dan shifted into position. "I'm good." Inch by inch the distance to the top shortened. Dan's fingers burned through his gloves, the arms reaching down to him not quite close enough. His muscles shook, and sweat dripped into his eyes. One more heave earned him precious inches, close enough for the reaching hands to pull Rebecca's weight off him. The team gave one final pull, dragging him over the top.

Rebecca lay on the ground well back from the edge. Sabrina sprawled on top of her, one blubbering mass. Dan had never seen a more beautiful sight.

Rebecca turned to him, Bree's cheek resting atop her own. He saw gratitude and something else he wouldn't let himself hope for. "Thank you for saving my baby," she whispered.

"And you mommy, he saved you too." Rebecca's hand came up slowly to stroke Sabrina's hair.

"Absolutely," she smiled. "Thank you for saving me too."

Sabrina whimpered when Kaden reached down to lift her off Rebecca. "We just need to check you over quickly sweetie, then your mom, to make sure she's all right. You can sit right here with Dan and hold her hand the entire time, okay?" Bree nodded.

Rebecca closed her eyes for the briefest of seconds. They opened again, clear and sure. She raised her hand to his face. "I never should have given you grief over something that wasn't your fault. I'm an idiot."

Dan turned his head, pressed her palm tightly against his mouth, and nodded. He could feel tears hanging on his eyelashes when he looked at her again. He didn't care.

"I love you, babe." He leaned over, brushing his lips over hers.

"I love you too," she said when his lips finally lifted.

Kaden pulled out a bottle of water and handed it to Sabrina, who then walked to Tricia and Emily, tugging on their hands to get them to follow her. Kaden must have checked them over already because they had water as well. Dan sat up and Bree dropped onto his crossed legs, reaching for her mother's hand. The girls sat beside them.

"Drink up sweetie." Kaden waited for Sabrina to comply before turning her attention to Rebecca." Sabrina looks good. A little dehydrated, but well. They'll do a more thorough check at the hospital, but she should be okay, physically. Now let's look at you."

"They gave me drugs, but they've mostly worn off now. I can probably walk out of here."

Dan laid his hand atop mother and daughter's. "Give it a few more minutes first. There's no rush now."

Rebecca felt her lip crack when she tried to smile. "What about the others?"

"They're taken care of, don't you be worrying about that now." Finn bent down and ruffled Sabrina's hair. "You have yourself one very courageous and resourceful child here." He leaned in to stroke the heads of the other two. "And her friends are pretty brave too."

Dan observed the girls, saw the way they watched the interplay between Rebecca and Bree. Tricia's emotions paraded across her face, the longing in her eyes to be back with her own mother obvious. He didn't envy the person to break the news that her parents were dead.

Emily's face told a different story. Her gaze held more curiosity, than wistfulness. When he looked at Emily, an old soul stared back. From what Ryker learned about Brad and Nora Banks, he imagined tender bonding moments hadn't happened very often in her short life.

Kaden finished bandaging Rebecca's head and helped her sit up. Bree switched laps as soon as Kaden gave the okay. Dan stood and walked over to the rest of the team, who were doing a good job of giving them space. Finn excluded, but then, that's Finn, and Dan wouldn't want any other wing man.

Evan nodded in Rebecca's direction. "As soon as Rebecca's ready we'll make our way out. Ryker called it in on his PRC. The place should be crawling with cops soon. As it is, we'll have to go through the scene to get to the entrance. It's not a scene any child should be seeing."

Emily's voice piped in behind them, her expression matter of fact. "I don't like the big room either. Bad things happen there. There's another tunnel that can take us to the exit."

Evan looked down at her. "Is there now? Why don't you show Ryker how we get to that other tunnel."

A few minutes later Rebecca insisted on standing up, and Dan helped her test her legs. She leaned heavily on him, but he figured she'd make it. Sabrina walked in front of them while Nick carried Tricia and stayed close to Bree. Emily impressed them all, taking the lead with Ryker, showing him the alternate route out without a single wrong turn.

Bains waited for them at the exit from the tunnels.

# Chapter Twenty-Eight

Controlled chaos met them at the entrance to the caves. Several choppers Law enforcement, Search and Rescue, and Medevac—sat a short distance away, doing what they could to light the area. The call for neighboring police forces to help went out, judging by the number of officers paired up with Society members, plus those trying to contain the scene.

One officer waved them over to the waiting Medevac. Two paramedics gently lifted Emily and Tricia into the chopper. Bree threw her arms around Rebecca, refusing to let go.

Dan crouched down to Bree's level. "They just need to look you over, make sure everything is okay. Don't worry. I won't let them leave without your mother. I promise."

Rebecca watched the scene playing out behind Dan, but looked down and cupped the back of Bree's head with her hand. "Go on sweetie, I'll be there in a minute. I need to talk to some people first, okay?"

Bree nodded but took her time unwrapping her arms from Rebecca's waist. Dan waited until the paramedics settled Bree in the chopper and distracted her before looking behind him. Rebecca put a hand on his arm.

"Oh, no you don't. He's mine." Rebecca covered the twenty-foot distance between her and Pete in about ten paces. "You bastard," she yelled. "Don't hide behind that cop you chicken shit coward. You don't deserve his protection Pete. You kidnapped and tortured children." All movement among the small crowd paused at the smack of her fist hitting his jaw. "You took your own daughter from her family." The shove knocked Pete to his knees. "You abused her." A well-placed kick to the ribs had Pete crying out and lunging behind a nearby officer, who held an arm out toward Rebecca in a half-hearted effort to halt her. "She trusted you to take care of her and you gave her to those monsters." The kick to his temple rolled his head back to the ground. "You're the lowest scumbag—" Rebecca fell to her knees, hands on her temples, "that exists."

"What's happening?" Dan shook her shoulders. "Talk to me, dammit."

Rebecca shook her head. "I don't know. I—" She doubled over with a gasp. The vision came through to her then.

*Pete in a bed, his naked shoulders bent over someone. He rolled to his side and Carrie's face appeared.*

"Leave her alone!" Bree shouted, her eyes piercing the shadows behind Pete, where a cry rang out. Rebecca's pain drifted away and she stood to watch Carrie stumble from the shadows, fingers clawing at her face. Her robes pooled around her when she fell to the ground, writhing.

Rebecca moved to go after her, but Dan's hands pulled her back. "Let Bains take care of Carrie. Bree needs you now." He turned Rebecca to face her daughter, seated on a patch of dirt, a bewildered paramedic standing next to her.

Rebecca fell to her knees and crushed Bree to her. "God baby, I'm sorry. So sorry. I should have known."

Bree pulled back, eyes clear and dry. Her small fingers gently brushed the tears from her mother's cheeks. "Don't worry mommy, I fixed it. Carrie can't hurt you anymore."

Rebecca turned to see several officers surrounding Carrie, who still writhed on the ground. Rebecca's eyes shot up to Dan until a soft melody had her turning back to Bree, who hummed a familiar tune.

She hugged Bree to her. "What are you doing, Bree"

"Making her hurt."

Rebecca frowned. "Where did you learn to do that?"

"The bad man who fell over the edge liked to practice on us. But he stopped when he found out that I can do it too."

You have to stop it now, sweetie, okay? Lift the pain off Carrie now." Carrie's agonized screams ceased, replaced by pitiful whimpers.

Bree pulled back and sat in the dirt humming the tune to Humpty Dumpty, her fingers methodically pleating the folds of her dress over and under.

# Chapter Twenty-Nine

Finn and Kaden caught up to Dan outside Sabrina's hospital room. Dan laughed at the three large stuffed animals Finn juggled and waved them in.

Finn dropped the toys on the empty bed and turned to Rebecca sitting in the chair next to it. "Everything all right with Sabrina?"

Kaden tapped Finn on the back of the head. "It's going to take a lot of therapy and love before she's close to all right again."

Rebecca gave Kaden a rueful smile. "For now, she's blocking a lot of it out. They're running final tests before they give the okay for her to come home." She grimaced. "My attendance is not required."

Dan laughed and rubbed his hand over her back. "The truth is they specifically asked her not to be there. Sabrina's a little clingy around Rebecca right now, understandably. It's easier for the staff if Rebecca waits here."

"And the sooner they're done the sooner you get to take her home." Kaden handed the book she held to Dan. "Thought you might want to turn this in to Chief Bains."

Dan nodded. "Thanks." He put the society's book on the table beside the bed. "Any new developments after we left yesterday?"

"We left the chief with more questions than answers, and he'll need that book for sure if he has a hope of making sense of this mess. For the moment he's occupied making room in his cells for everyone."

"Any other casualties?"

Kaden shook her head. "Just Joshua and the guy he took with him, Norman Parks. The rest of them have light concussions and a few bruises, a lot less then they deserve. The chief's pissed at the number of people in his town who managed to outsmart him for so long. I'm afraid that bunch is going to bear the brunt of it." Kaden smiled. "As they should. How are you doing Rebecca?"

"Better now that it's over." She wiped a tear away and gave a watery laugh. "I'm sorry. I thought I finished crying."

Dan touched the white bandage circling Rebecca's head. "Rebecca will be fine. Her head took a hard hit on that ledge, but thanks to your care at the scene, suffered minimal blood loss. The drugs are entirely out of her system now and the doc's released her. She'll go home when Sabrina does."

"That's great news."

Dan raised his eyebrow when Finn sat against the edge of the bed and leaned down to chair height to kiss the top of her head. He leaned out of the way, as Dan went to smack him, earning a chuckle out of Rebecca.

"It's good to hear you laughing again. And by the looks of things you've decided to forgive this big lout." Finn winked. "If you've an inclination to change your mind, you just let me know."

Dan shoved him off the bed. When they all stopped laughing Kaden picked up two of the animals. "We'd like to drop these off to Tricia and Emily, and then we need to get going. We're sorry we missed Sabrina. We'll come and visit once you've had a chance to settle in at home."

Rebecca stood and gave both of them a hug. "I don't know how to thank you."

"Knowing you and the lass are together again is all we need."

Rebecca smiled as they left, thinking of the birthday cake she'd make for Bree this year. They'd finally get to eat it together.

She tugged on Dan's hand. "Come on, let's walk a bit. I need to do something or I'll go crazy." They found Susan Henry, the CPS agent assigned to Emily and Tricia, at the nurses' station.

"How are the girls doing?" Dan wrapped his arm behind Rebecca's waist.

Dark circles under Susan's eyes attested to her exhaustion. "Tricia doesn't understand. She wants to go home to her parents. The psychologists want us to wait a bit before telling her there's no one to go home to. She's so young, she'll be okay eventually. Emily is—well, distant I guess is the word I'd use. I'm more concerned about her."

"Can we see them?"

Susan shook her head. "I'd rather you not at this time. I ran into your friends and gave the girls their gifts on their behalf. The psychologist wants to limit contact with anyone who might trigger memories of what happened. He wants to have a few sessions with them first." She shrugged her shoulders. "After that, we'll take it day by day."

"Have any family come forward?" Rebecca asked.

Dan looked at Susan, and then away.

"What?" Rebecca broke in.

Dan sighed. "They can't release either of them to family, even if someone came forward. This cult spread through generations of families. Everyone is suspect and will have to be thoroughly investigated."

"That could take months." Rebecca turned troubled eyes to Susan. "What will happen to the girls, where will they go?"

"Foster care. I'll do my best to place them together but I have to be honest, that's usually not possible in situations like this. First off, they aren't siblings. And these two will need a lot of counseling and patience. Most families find one special needs child emotionally draining. Taking in two is asking a lot of our foster parents."

Rebecca swung her gaze to Dan, then back to Susan at his answering smile. "What do I need to do to become a foster parent?"

Susan's smile broadened. They walked with her to the elevator as they discussed the process. She left with a plan and promises to get things moving as soon as possible. Rebecca crossed her fingers that CPS would recognize the bond the girls had developed, and see the benefits of keeping them together.

"You need to rest," Dan said when Rebecca dropped down in the chair in Bree's room.

"I'll rest when this is over." She relented when an argument formed on Dan's lips. "When I bring Bree home, we'll snuggle up together in my bed and sleep the rest of the day if that will make you happy." She glared at her watch. "It's been almost an hour."

Dan moved behind her chair and massaged her shoulders. "I can think of something to pass the time." He leaned down to nuzzle her neck. She turned her head and caught his smile with her lips.

The sound of a throat clearing broke them apart.

"Chief." Dan walked around to shake his hand.

"I hoped I could speak to Sabrina."

"Is that necessary?" Rebecca frowned. "I'd be happy to answer any questions you have, but I don't want my daughter to have to relive that nightmare."

"I have questions for you too, both of you, but I'm afraid I'll need a statement from Sabrina first hand. If you think she's uncomfortable, at any time, I'll stop. It's best to get this over with as soon as possible," he said at her continued frown. "Then Sabrina can put it behind her and get on with the business of healing."

Rebecca sighed, but nodded.

The chief hooked his thumbs in his waistband. "It's quite the mess you uncovered here. I'll be doing paperwork for weeks." He caught her look of disdain. "I'm sorry I didn't have more faith when you came in for updates on the search." He shook his head. "This is one time I'm happy to be proven wrong."

Rebecca nodded. It's hard to match a mother's faith.

"If the two of you can come in to see me in the next couple of days that should do just fine," Bains said, as the orderly wheeled Sabrina into the room. She squealed at the sight of the giant panda on the bed, and stared at the chief as Dan settled her under the covers.

Rebecca sat next to Bree and held the hand that wasn't strangling the panda. She smiled down at Sabrina. "Bree honey, this is Chief Bains and he'd like to ask you a few questions, if you feel up to it. Would that be okay?"

Bree looked to her mother. "Is it okay with you?"

Rebecca nodded.

"Okay."

Bains pulled the chair up and sat at Sabrina's level. I know you've been through a lot, so if you want me to stop at any time, just say so. Okay?" Bree nodded. "If I showed you pictures of some people, do you think you'd be able to tell me if any of them were involved in taking you and keeping you and the other children?" Bree nodded again. "Did they do anything to hurt you?" When Bree stiffened beside her, Rebecca opened her mouth to protest.

Sabrina took a deep breath. "It's okay, mommy," she said, looking at the chief. "The doctors already asked me if they hurt me, but they didn't. Except for the tattoo, but they did that while I was asleep from the pills. I didn't like the pills they gave me. And they were kinda mean, mostly."

"Did you stay in the caves the whole time?"

She shook her head. "Mostly, but we stayed in a house sometimes too."

"When you stayed in the house, did the people wear their cloaks and hoods?"

She looked down. "Only for the ceremonies."

Dan looked to the chief, who shook his head. "How do you know they wore cloaks at the ceremonies, Sabrina?"

Her arms tightened on the neck of the panda. Her voice lowered, barely audible. "They made us watch."

"Dear god." Rebecca's free hand few to her mouth. She tried to stay strong for Bree's sake, but couldn't stop the tears from flowing down her face.

"That's enough, Chief." Dan interrupted, and Bains nodded. "They can't do this right now. It's too soon. You should have plenty of evidence at the scene. Everyone involved is accounted for. We found a book, some kind of bible for the cult. You should find a lot of your answers in there." Dan cursed when he saw the empty table.

"Dan left it right there," Rebecca said. "Dan, check with the nurses and see if anyone came in to clean while we stepped out."

"I'm sorry if my questions upset you and your mom, Sabrina. Maybe we can talk again another time, when you're feeling up to it." Dan walked the chief out, stopping at the nurses' station just outside the door of the room. Bains nodded at Dan in agreement to something, but didn't look too happy about it. With a final nod, Bains left, and Dan came back in the room, followed by Sabrina's doctor.

He smiled at Sabrina. "Well young lady, how do you feel about going home?"

# Chapter Thirty

Rebecca celebrated Bree's progress every day, but knew they had a long way to go. The scars remained and may never heal, the tattoo among the least of them. Bree saw her therapist twice, once with Rebecca and once on her own. Dr. Randall impressed upon them strength, resilience, and time were the key to addressing most of her issues.

She also stressed that much of Bree's anger would dissipate over time, but the feelings of betrayal toward her father may never go away. When Rebecca mentioned her plan to take in Tricia and Emily as foster kids, Dr. Randall hesitated, saying she'd like to witness the bond herself before making a recommendation. Either way, Bree and Rebecca had plenty of therapy sessions ahead of them.

Dan stayed the first night, bunking on the sleeper sofa, while Bree snuggled in with her. He left the next morning, to give her and Bree some time to get to know one another again, he explained. But enough was enough. Rebecca called him this morning, after a week-long absence, demanding he get his butt back where it belonged. She looked at her watch and grinned when she heard his car pull in. He made the hour long drive in forty minutes.

Running to the side of the house, she met him half way, leapt into his arms, and wrapped her legs around his waist. He hooked his hands under her bottom and grinned. A few minutes later, she came up for air.

"God, I've missed you." She laughed and kissed him again. "I feel like it's been a month, instead of a week."

She lowered her legs with reluctance and laced her fingers with his. "Bree's on the swing-set."

He stopped before they came into sight. "How's she doing?"

Rebecca smiled. "Better every day. Still has bad moments, but as long as we don't turn out the lights, she sleeps through the night. She's finally moved back to her own bed. Apparently I'm too restless—said she had to move back to her own bed to get any sleep."

Dan laughed. "Smart kid."

"She asked about you?"

"Did you explain why I left?"

"Yes, but that's not what I meant. She asked what your favorite color is and about your favorite food, movie, and game, that sort of thing."

"Blue. Pasta of any kind. National Lampoon's Christmas Vacation. Scrabble."

Rebecca leaned in and rested her head on his chest. "You know what this means don't you?" she asked, pulling back to look at him. He shook his head. "She likes you," Rebecca answered.

He smiled and tucked a strand of hair escaping her ponytail behind her ear. "She's pretty remarkable. Like her mother." He took his time with this kiss, pulling back to nibble at her lips, then sinking in again. His hands went to her hips and pressed her close. Her abdomen contracted at the hard ridge struggling to escape the front of his jeans.

"Mommy, who's here?" Dan pulled away and moved around the corner.

"It's Dan sweetie." She smiled when he reappeared, shirt tails untucked.

Bree smiled at him. "Hi. I'm glad you're back, my mom missed you."

"I missed her too."

"Are you going to stick around longer this time?"

Dan smiled and looked at Rebecca. "That depends on your mom. And you."

"Oh, she wants you to stay. She thinks about you all the time, and she has dreams of you."

Rebecca looked at her daughter. "What makes you say that?"

"I can see in your dreams. Can we have tacos for dinner? Great," she said at Rebecca's nod and ran back to her swing set.

"Well that's a little disconcerting." She sat on the bench on the back porch and pulled Dan down with her.

"What? That she would have some kind of psychic ability. You're always telling me it's more common than people think."

"Well yeah, of course. But seeing my dreams? The kinds of dreams I've been having about you are not something I want my daughter seeing." He leaned down and whispered in her ear in very explicit detail the dream she wished she had. She fanned her face with her hand.

"If you two are gonna keep that up you should go inside." Bree stood right in front of them.

Rebecca and Dan broke apart, putting as much distance between them as the small bench allowed. They looked at each other, and then at Bree and burst out laughing.

Rebecca pulled Bree onto her lap. "I'm sorry honey, I'm just so happy to have my two favorite people here with me." She shifted Bree so she could meet her eyes. "You know, it's not polite to visit people's dreams, sweetheart." She had a sudden thought. "Is it just my dreams you visit, or can you visit other people too?" She felt more than heard Dan's intake of breath. He got her point.

"Just you mommy." Both Rebecca and Dan exhaled in relief. "But I can hear most anyone when they're awake. Ever since I went to the caves, I can do a lot of things. The chief taught me how."

"Chief Bains?" Dan looked at Rebecca.

"No silly, the Indian chief. He's Apache. He didn't like what those people did in the mines. He tried to make sure people stayed out." She looked at Dan. "You saw him. He showed you which tunnel to take to get to mommy."

Dan looked at Rebecca. "I never told anyone about that. I'd pretty much convinced myself it hadn't happened."

"You're not losing your mind," Bree said to Dan.

Dan stood up. "This mind reading thing of yours is going to take some getting used to."

Rebecca debated between dealing with Bree and grilling Dan about this vision. With a sigh, she turned to Bree. "It's not polite to visit people's minds either. Thoughts are private, that's why they're in our heads. When we want you to know what we're thinking we'll tell you. That's how it works. Understood?"

Bree nodded. "I'm sorry mommy. Most times, I don't even know I'm doing it. I'll try harder."

Rebecca gave her a hug. "Thank you sweetie, that's all I can ask."

Dan knelt down to face her. "What else did this Indian chief teach you?"

"He talked to me with the wind. He was angry the day you saved mommy."

"Angry with us?"

"Oh no. With the bad man who fell over the edge. And the others too. He liked you guys. He used the wind to help hold the ledge up so mommy wouldn't fall."

"Well, that's quite something." Dan looked at Rebecca. "I appreciated his help." Dan cleared his throat. "There's something else I've been meaning to ask you. Right before I rappelled down to get your mother you told her to do something, do you remember?"

She shrugged her shoulder. "Sure, I told her do what you said for once."

"What made you say that sweetie?" Rebecca asked.

"Because he told you to stay at Ruby's and you left. You should've listened to him mommy."

Rebecca's mouth dropped open. "Did you see me the whole time you were gone?"

"No, only when you were with him." She pointed to Dan.

"Me? Why me?"

"Because of your powers."

Dan shook his head. "I don't have any powers."

"Yes you do, silly."

"When did you first see Dan, do you remember?"

"The day he sat on my bed, thinking real hard. He kind of jumped out and surprised me. I tried hard to talk to him, but he's got a thick head."

Rebecca hid her smile. "Were you at the house or the caves when this happened?"

"The caves."

"There's a legend about the Peaks and their ability to bring out paranormal abilities," Rebecca explained to Dan. "Many psychics who visit claim their gifts are enhanced while there." She shrugged. "I've never experienced it myself, but it could explain why Bree came into her gift when she did."

"Can I ask a question now?" Bree's expression grew thoughtful, her lips puckered like a cherub.

"Of course."

"When you two get married can I be the flower girl? I always wanted to be a flower girl. And after all, he's marrying me too."

"Um…" Rebecca bit her lip and looked at Dan.

He scooped Bree up. "Absolutely you can. When do you want to get married?"

"Tomorrow?"

"Hmm. Tomorrow would be nice, but we'll need time to pick out a pretty dress for you. How about sometime after your birthday? Next month maybe?

"Sure, I like October too. That's when Halloween is."

"October it is." He kissed her on the cheek and set her down

"Now you gotta ask mommy."

"Bree…"

Dan hoisted Bree up and sat her on the bench next to her mother. He got down on one knee. "Sabrina Eileen and Rebecca Mary McKenney, will you marry me?"

Bree bounced where she sat and clapped her hands. "Oh, yes," she said. "I'll marry you." She leaped into her mother's arms. "You're not supposed to cry mommy, this is supposed to happen. He did it exactly right and everything."

Rebecca laughed, hugged her daughter, and then wiped a tear from her lashes. "Well then, if he did it exactly right, I'd better say yes."

"Hurray, we're getting married." She ran toward her swing-set, but stopped before she reached it, and then came back. She tugged on Dan's hand until he bent down, and then whispered in his ear. He smiled and patted his pocket. "Thank you, but I've got it covered." She clapped her hands again and ran off.

"What did she say?"

"She said it's all right that I forgot the ring. And she'd help me pick out the perfect one if I'd like."

Rebecca took pity on Dan. "Just because she says so, doesn't make it true."

"You said yes. There's no backing out now."

"Dan I know you'd do anything for my daughter, but you don't have to marry me because she asked you to."

He picked her up and sat down with her in his lap. He tilted a bit and reached into his pocket. "How about if I want to?"

Rebecca's mouth flapped open and closed, but no sound came out.

"I love you Rebecca. I love your determination and spirit, your sense of humor. I love the way you're a sore loser at games and you rub it in when you win." He brushed his lips over hers and whispered in her ear. "The way you bite your lip when you're nervous makes me want to rip your clothes off." He leaned back and rubbed his fingers over her face. "I love the freckles on your cheeks." His hand dipped to caress her abdomen. "And here. I love that miniature you over there on the swing-set. I love the way you look at me, the way you make me feel. I love everything about you." He reached down and picked up the box on the seat beside him. She hadn't even noticed it until now. He opened the box and turned it to her. The box held a white gold band with two channel set diamonds. "Rebecca Mary McKenney, will you share your life, your daughter, and your heart with me for the rest of our lives?"

She traced a shaking finger over the band. "Two diamonds?"

"One for you, one for Sabrina."

"Oh god."

"Is that a yes?"

"Yes." Her hand shook so bad he could barely slide the ring on her finger. "You're my soul mate Dan. When Joshua took me all I thought about was Bree, you, and how much you'd be worrying. How stupid I'd been to leave Ruby's." She wiped her tears on the edge of his shirt. "But I never doubted you'd find me." She took his hand and placed it over her heart. "I could feel you here." She giggled.

"What's so funny?"

"I'm really hoping Sabrina is doing what I told her and not peeking into my thoughts right now."

Dan's eyes darkened as he brought his hand up to frame her face. She moaned, when he moved his lips to the hollow of her throat, and wiggled her bottom in his lap.

"If you do that again I'm going to explode right here on the bench."

Rebecca went still for a moment then wiggled again. His hands moved to her hips, held her in place, pressing down. She watched the struggle to hold it together on his face.

"Will you two go inside already? Geesh."

They both burst out laughing. Dan stood, lifting Rebecca with him. "What are you doing?"

"My future daughter told me to go inside if I want to kiss her mother."

"Put me down now." Rebecca smacked his arm and laughed when he let her legs swing to the ground. She wrapped her arms around his waist and rested her head on his chest while she watched Sabrina hang upside down from the bar on the swing-set. She had her daughter back. She had Dan. She brought his hand up and pressed a kiss to the back. She had her life back. A life she was ready to start living again.

# About the Author

S. J. Clarke has published over fifty articles as a columnist and regular contributor for a variety of lifestyle and human interest websites. She is a grateful member of the Writers' Community of Durham Region, and proud to sit on the Board of Directors for The Ontario Writer's Conference. Sandra also co-authored Touretties, a touching tribute featuring testimonials from patients and their loved ones living with Tourettes. Mind Over Matter is her first novel.

CPSIA information can be obtained at www.ICGtesting.com
Printed in the USA
LVOW090751251111

256337LV00003B/4/P